CAPE COD
A NEIGHBOR'S MURDER

11/18/17
To Sarah,
Enjoy the read!
Roberta Schneiderman

CAPE COD
A NEIGHBOR'S MURDER

A NOVEL

ROBERTA SCHNEIDERMAN

Salty Pilgrim Press
A Division of Parker-Nelson Publishing
Millis, Massachusetts

ISBN 978-1935616115

This is a work of fiction. Names, characters, places, and incidents are the product of the author's imagination or are used fictitiously. Any similarity to real persons, living or dead, is coincidental and not intended by the author.

I would like to thank the following people . . .

My first readers—Jason Brooks, Barbara Jablon, Diane Kwatcher, and Rona Davis all of whom took the time to read my very rough draft and offer helpful suggestions.

My designer, Linda Humphrey, who outdid herself once again and created a truly beautiful cover

My editor, Jean Kirshenbaum, whose knowledge and keen eye helped to polish this book.

My publisher, Ted Burbank, who has been there for me every step of the way.

And finally, my husband, Herb Schneiderman, who has the patience of a saint.

To the readers who asked me to write a sequel to my book *Cape Cod – Murder at a Gated Community*, I thank you for your encouragement and support.

CAPE COD
A NEIGHBOR'S MURDER

CHAPTER 1

Cape Cod was in the middle of Hurricane Sandy. It was predicted to hit most of the Northeast and Mid-Atlantic states even though hurricane season was supposed to be over. Large portions of the Cape were without power. Judy had set out emergency lanterns and was listening to news reports on her battery-operated radio. All sources said this would be a significant storm, so she and Phil planned to monitor their families in Boston and New York. She also planned to keep an eye on their neighbor Mary.

Judy yelled to Phil who was upstairs in his office. "I think I'll call Mary and check on her."

"Leave her alone," Phil yelled back. "You've already spoken to her a million times today. She'll call you if she needs you."

Judy was bored. She was tired of listening to storm predictions on the radio, running back and forth to the window, and trying to read her book. She had waited weeks for the best seller, and now she couldn't concentrate. "What are you doing upstairs?" she shouted once more. He had developed wife deafness, so she shouted when he was in his office because she hated to be ignored.

"I'm cleaning the top of my desk so you'll stop hounding me not that my desk is any of your concern." Before Phil's retirement, the clutter on his desk was a constant irritation to his boss, who would ask Phil how he ever found anything. That was the funny part. Phil always found what he needed in his piles of papers and assorted junk. Judy, on the other hand, who prided herself on her neatness, could never find what she needed on her desk.

Now that Phil was busy at his desk, Judy decided to check on Mary. If he commented, she would say he had not heard her say she was going next door for some company.

Mary had moved to the gated community of Northridge the previous year. She was several years older than Judy, but the two of them connected immediately.

Judy's mother had died several years earlier, and Judy missed her. They had been very close. Her mother had even lived with them during the summer months when it became too hot for her to stay in Florida. Mary, who lived alone, seemed to fill the vacuum in Judy's life. Because Mary had no relatives, they soon became like mother and daughter. Judy was more comfortable with Mary than Phil was. He said she was too clingy, but Judy seemed to enjoy the relationship. One episode particularly bothered Phil. It had taken place about a month earlier . . .

"Judy," said Phil, "that was Mary on the phone. She wants to know if you can come over. Says she has something to give you."

Judy had been in the bathroom when the phone rang. Usually she answered. Phil hated to talk on the phone, and it was usually for her anyway.

"What did you tell her?" Judy asked.

"What do you think? I said you'd call her back. I don't answer for you although you seem to always answer for me."

Judy groaned inwardly. She was not going to let him aggravate her or get her to bite. She knew half the time it was a game he played to see if he could get to her. So she ignored his comments and called Mary.

"Hi, it's me. What's up?"

"Honey, if you aren't busy, could you come over for a bit. I need to discuss something with you. Are you busy? I mean if you and Phil are busy, it can wait for another time. You know how I hate to bother you."

"Mary, you aren't bothering me," Judy said. "I've finished folding laundry and taking a shower, and we aren't meeting our friends at Bleu for a couple of hours. I can come over now." Bleu was one of Judy and Phil's favorite restaurants. The chef and owner used to run a restaurant in New York, and he had brought some real upscale dining to the area. Judy and Phil loved the food and tried to go there a few times a month. Retirement and cooking were not always a good match for Judy. Retirement and restaurants seemed to be a much better fit.

"Thanks Judy," she said. "It can wait, but something has been on my mind. You know how I need to do everything the minute I think of it."

"I know that, Mary; no need to apologize. I'm the same way," Judy said. "Hey Phil, I'm going next door to Mary. I won't be long."

"That's no big surprise," Phil said. "When Mary calls, Judy jumps."

"Cheap shot Phil. You're better than that. She's all alone, and she thinks of us as her family. And besides, sometimes she feels like a mother to me."

"That's pretty strange having no family, don't you think?" "Who doesn't have family or at least close friends. Christ, with technology today, everyone has connections all over the place."

"Yah, yah. I'll be back in time to get dressed," and she left and knocked on Mary's door.

"Come in, come in, Honey. It's open as usual."

Even though the door was unlocked, Judy always

knocked. "Mary, why do you leave your door open? It's not a good idea. You should keep it locked. Phil and I even keep our car locked when it's not in the garage. It's just a good habit."

"Oh Honey, you worry about me too much. It's just easier to keep it unlocked. That way I don't have to carry a key when I'm out or jump up when someone rings the bell. With this arthritis, getting up off the sofa can be a little painful. I hope you never have to deal with arthritis. And besides, the guard at the gate always calls if someone is here to see me. So don't worry."

"I do worry," Judy said. "I worry about you being alone," and she walked over and gave Mary a hug. "You know how much our friendship means to me," Judy said.

"And you have become my family, Judy, the family I never had. Now sit down and talk to me. I made us some tea, and I have those delicious cookies you always get me when you go to Trader Joes."

"Just one cookie, Mary. Remember we're going out to dinner tonight, and I want to save my calories for a big gooey dessert."

"Okay, just one cookie. I put a sugar in your tea and let it cool down a little. It's the way you like it."

"Thank you Mary. Now what did you want to tell me?"

"You know I'm fine, Honey. In fact I haven't felt this good in a long time, so I wanted to have this talk before anything happened to me."

"What do you mean? What might happen to you?" Judy said.

"Nothing's going to happen to me, but I'm not getting any younger. At my age no one knows what the next day might bring. I wanted to talk to you and give you a letter. I want you to put it in a safe place along with this box. If anything happens, like if I die, you know what I mean, open the letter first. It'll explain what's in the box. It will all belong to you then, and whatever you decide to do with the letter and the contents of the box will be the correct decision."

"Mary, you're scaring me," Judy said. "Do you have a premonition? Are you entrusting me with something valuable? You know we've talked before about trying to locate your family. With today's internet searches, it shouldn't be too hard."

"I know you mean well, Judy, but there's no one I care to contact and no one who would care about me. The contents of the box and the letter are valuable but not in a monetary way. Tuck them away and forget about them. I hope you don't have to open them for years."

"Oh Mary, you know I'd do anything for you. But, you're frightening me."

"Nonsense, Honey. It's fine. Now let's have a little visit before you have to leave."

When Judy got home and showed the letter and box to Phil, he became agitated.

"Something's a little out of joint with your friend Mary. No family, no friends, and now a mystery letter and a mystery box. I don't like it."

"You don't have to like it," she said. "There's nothing to like or not like. She's my friend, and I enjoy her company. She simply asked me to hold a letter and a box. It's probably some stuff with sentimental value. It's no big deal. I don't know why I even mentioned it. I should have known you'd have something negative to say."

"Don't be so sensitive," Phil said. "Go get dressed before we're late. You know how I hate to be late."

Judy wanted to go to dinner, otherwise she would have put him in his place and maybe even stormed out of the house. She put the letter and the box in a safe place and proceeded to get dressed.

The incident happened weeks earlier, and Judy forgot

about it until the night's tragic discovery.

The temperature in the house had dropped dramatically without the power. So, before heading to see Mary, Judy pulled out a couple of extra blankets. Suddenly the windows rattled, the intensity of the rain and wind increased, and all hell broke loose. There was a crash, and Judy screamed.

"What the hell was that?" Phil hollered as he barreled down the stairs. "Judy, are you okay? What in the world? Oh crap! I bet we lost that big tree out front."

Judy followed him to the front window. A huge tree was across their car, or what used to be their car.

"Oh my God Phil!" Judy cried out. "We could have been killed if that tree landed on the house. At least we weren't hurt." Judy could feel herself tremble. There had not been a serious hurricane in the area for years, and the fallen tree had shaken her.

"I'm going out to see if that oak did any other damage beyond killing our car," said Phil. "We'll probably have to wait a long time to get this cleaned."

"I hope it won't be too long. What a mess. I think I'll go out too and check on Mary." She grabbed her raincoat.

This time he did not argue, but he did tell her to be careful when she skirted around the tree and made her way next door. Living in their condo community meant neighbors were only steps from one another.

Judy quickly opened Mary's door to get out of the rain and wind. This time she did not knock. Besides, with the howling wind, in addition to the torrential rain, Mary probably would not have heard her. "Mary, it's Judy," she yelled. "Did that crash scare you? I came over to make sure you were okay. Mary, are you in the bedroom? It's Judy." Hearing no response, she decided to open the door and wondered why Mary would have closed it. What if Mary had fallen? She had been after Mary to get one of those alert bracelets, but Mary always insisted she did not need one. Judy's heart was racing, but she tried to remain calm as she turned the knob. She was startled to see Mary's chair and desk overturned, her bedding in a heap on the floor, and her bureau drawers upended. Judy panicked. She quickly opened the bathroom door and then screamed. Mary was in the tub. Her body sprawled and bloodied. Judy screamed a second time and ran out of the house, nearly losing her footing as she rounded the downed tree. She rushed to find Phil, unable to stop screaming and crying.

"Judy! What the hell's going on? Stop crying. I can't understand a word you're saying. You're scaring the shit out of me. What's wrong? Is it Mary? What is it?"

"Yes, no, I don't know," she gasped. "Oh God! What happened? What happened to her? Phil, it's Mary." And Judy began to choke as she tried to calm down enough to answer Phil. "Phil, she's dead! She's in her bathtub. There's so much blood. Phil she's dead! I think someone killed her! Phil, who would do that to Mary?" Judy grabbed Phil's hand and yelled, "Please hurry, hurry! Maybe she's still alive."

Phil snatched his raincoat and followed Judy to Mary's house. "Careful," he yelled and yanked her back as a large branch fell onto their flowerbed. "Take my hand and be careful where you walk. You can't help Mary if you get hurt. Now what do you want me to see? Where's Mary?"

She held on to him for dear life and dragged him into Mary's bathroom.

"What the hell!" he yelled. "Don't touch anything. Is this the way you found her?" Judy could only nod. Mary was naked, there was blood everywhere, and it looked like her throat had been slit. "We need to call the police. Don't touch anything," he yelled again. "Let's get out of here. Who would kill an old lady like that? None of this makes sense. Quick, grab my hand and watch your step. We need to get the police over here right away."

Judy sobbed as they ran back to the house. The car crushed by the tree was now the last thing on their minds.

"Where's your cell?" asked Phil. "Mine's dead." He was shaking as he grabbed Judy's cell off the hall table. "I'll put the phone on speaker, but let me talk. You're almost incoherent, and they need to understand what's going on here."

She agreed and listened while Phil tried to explain what they had seen at Mary's house. She thought he was amazingly clear, but she could not believe the police response.

"I'm sorry Mr. Weinberger. Give me your address and please spell your last name. I'll send over the first cruiser I can get, and please don't touch a thing. We'll get there as soon as possible, but we're overwhelmed here due to the hurricane. We're getting calls for help from all over town. The storm has created havoc over at the beach, shore road is flooded, and we're trying to move folks from the assisted living complex to the high school because they've lost their back-up generator. We have accidents all over the place, and a few fires have started as a result of downed lines. We've even got a cruiser down crushed by a tree. Hold tight, and again, don't touch anything over there. Lock your door, and don't let anyone in but one of our officers. We'll get to you as soon as we can." And he hung up.

"What are we going to do?" Judy said between sobs. "We can't leave her there. Oh my God Phil, I can't believe the police aren't coming right over. Don't they understand what happened? This is too awful. Who would do such a thing? Why would anyone want to kill Mary? Oh no, I think I'm going to be sick," and she ran into the bathroom and got rid of her dinner, her lunch, and probably everything from the past few days before beginning to dry heave. Phil followed her into the bathroom.

"Try to get up," he whispered. "Sit over here and breathe slowly. You're fine; you're just scared. I wish I could throw up myself. I feel like someone hit me in the gut. We'll figure this out. The murderer certainly picked a good time. He must have realized the storm would help cover his tracks. We have to stay calm and wait until the police arrive. I'm sure they'll be able to figure it out. All we can do is wait. Do you still feel like you're going to throw up?"

"I think I'm . . . Phil, Mary's letter and box!" she gasped. "She gave them to me and said to open them if anything happened to her. Do you think she suspected something? Phil, we have to get them. We have to see what they say. They're down stairs in the cellar on the table in the back room. Hurry!"

Phil returned with both items and placed them on the dining room table. Judy tore open the letter and, with shaking hands, read it aloud . . .

Dear Judy,

You've been like a daughter to me and the love of my life this past year. I have never known such peace, and I thank you and Phil for your friendship, your kindness, and your love.

Either you're reading this because I died of natural causes or someone found me after all these years. I've not always been the person you've come to know, and you wouldn't have associated with me had you known me in my other life. I've done immoral and scandalous things, and I've broken the law countless times. I've hidden my real identity since I first left home. I've been known by many different names, but I've always managed to stay under the radar. Details are in the diaries in the box I gave you. After reading all of them, you can give everything to the police or you can destroy this letter, the diaries, and the contents of the box. It's your choice. You're wise and will know what to do. Read the diaries from beginning to end. That will help you understand everything.

Don't grieve for me. I don't deserve it. I wasn't a very nice person. You brought out the best in me. I only wish I had come to know you earlier in my life. I loved you Judy more than I have ever loved anyone. I wish you and Phil a long and healthy life with your beautiful children and grandchildren. You only deserve the best.
With much love,
Mary

"I don't believe what I'm reading. I can't believe this, Phil," said Judy who reread the letter several more times to make sure she understood what Mary was telling her.

"I knew it! I knew there was something that didn't add up about your friend," said Phil. "And you call yourself a good judge of character. For heaven's sake, she was a guest in our house a million times; she ate at our table; you were always alone with her; she was in the house with our grandkids. This is crazy! Judy, why aren't you saying something? Why are you so quiet? That's not like you; you always have a comment about everything. What do you think of my suspicions now? Who's the better judge of character now!"

"Be quiet!" she yelled. "Now's not the time to lecture me. I don't understand any of this. She was always so kind, so sweet, so caring. Does that sound like the description of a bad person to you? For God's sake, I always thought people who broke the law were horrible people. Maybe she had a reason for calling herself by different names. Maybe she meant something else by it."

"Right," Phil snickered. "She meant to say she was a former nun, but she chose the wrong words. Grow up Judy.

She's a criminal by her own admission, and now we're involved in a police investigation. Boy, you do know how to pick your friends. First we're involved in Jerry Smith's murder investigation, and now it's another of your wonderful friends. You're getting better; this one's a real criminal off the bat. Next thing I know you'll somehow be friends with a terrorist."

"Why are you so mean? Jerry wasn't my friend. Susan was. Susan was his victim, and justice was served when he was killed. This is different, and you know it. Mary didn't bother anyone. She was kind and sweet, and everyone liked her."

"Yup," Phil answered sarcastically. "I bet her victims all loved her. Maybe their families would like to come to her funeral and speak loving words about her. Maybe you can even start a scholarship in her name at the high school."

"If you're finished aggravating me, let's see what's in that box and then decide what we're going to say and do when the police arrive."

"What we're going to say and do when the police arrive! Are you crazy? Are we going to conspire to hinder a police investigation by not disclosing the existence of that letter and that box? Are you sure you aren't on drugs? Your reasoning's a little wacky I think."

"Stop yelling at me. Why do you always yell?" Judy had stopped crying, and anger at her husband was becoming her prevailing emotion. "Mary asked me to read her letter, check out the contents of the box, and then decide what to do. We've read her letter; now be quiet so we can check out what's in the box."

Judy went into the kitchen, felt her way around the inside of the junk drawer, and finally found the razor she always used for opening packages. Living without power was proving to be a challenge.

"Come in the kitchen," she said, "and bring the box

with you. Do you think I should lay out some paper towels or a newspaper and handle this box with my rubber gloves so we don't mess up any fingerprints?"

"Yes and yes," Phil said. "I think we should be careful how we touch whatever is in the box. I wish the police would hurry up and come. Then there wouldn't be any question about turning the evidence over, not that there's any question in my mind."

"Look Phil," she said a little surprised. "There's a ton of notebooks in here. Mary told me she kept a diary. And look, they're numbered and dated. The one on the top is dated last month. If we're going to decide what to do, I think we should begin with the oldest notebook, like Mary said in her letter."

"I think we should begin with the most recent one so we can see if there are any clues about who murdered her," Phil said. "Maybe she suspected something. If we don't find anything, we can always go back to the beginning."

"That makes sense," said Judy. "We'll get through this together; just be patient, and don't snap at me." To her surprise, Phil gave her a hug and said okay.

"Why don't I read the last few entries aloud so we're both hearing the same information," said Judy. "It's probably easier for me to read Mary's handwriting than it is for you to try and figure it out. She's been scribbling grocery lists for me for a long time."

"Sure," Phil said. "I'll move the lantern to the sofa, so I can look on with you. We can call it great reading for a stormy night."

"You promised not to be sarcastic," groaned Judy. "We haven't even started, and you're at it again."

"Sorry," said Phil. "Where's the first entry? We better get moving if you want to get through some of this before the police get here."

Judy pulled out the newest diary and opened it to

Mary's most recent entry. The page was dated earlier in the month. As she read, she could see Phil's eyes rolling. He was bored and rightly so. She was simply reading about Mary's everyday events. Judy wondered if it made any sense to continue reading aloud since she was putting Phil to sleep. She didn't have to wonder for long.

"This isn't getting us anywhere," he said. "Go back a few more weeks."

Judy read the part Phil suggested, but it continued to bore him. "I have an idea," she said. "I can go through this much faster if I don't have to read aloud. If I find anything that makes me think there's something here, I'll read it to you." He agreed. "And," she said, "if the police come before I have a chance to get a handle on these diaries, promise me you won't say anything about them. We can always say they were in the cellar, but we never thought about them because we were in shock about Mary."

"Oh right," Phil answered sarcastically. "Now you want me to assist in a cover-up. I already said we should turn everything over to the police. Besides, you aren't an investigator; you aren't a detective. How do you know if what you're reading is important or not? Answer that one for me."

"You're being mean again," Judy said while fighting back tears. "Mary was my friend, and I was obviously very important to her. She gave all of this to me. She trusted me with the letter and the diaries. She said that I was to decide what to do. She didn't say you were to decide. In fact she didn't even say you and I should decide. She didn't even say I should share this information with you. I wanted to go over it with you, but now I've changed my mind. So just forget that I have the letter and the diaries. Forget what you learned when I read that letter aloud. I'm going to go through the diaries from the very beginning. That's the only way they'll make sense. That's what Mary wanted me to do. If I come across anything I think the police should know, I'll call my friend Detective Partridge and ask for his advice. What are they going to do, arrest me? I can say I thought they were personal diaries, and I didn't realize they might be related to her murder until I read them. So when the police come, don't say anything. It's my decision."

Judy could tell Phil was furious. He stormed out of the room, grabbed his raincoat, and went to check on his car and the downed tree. The rain had abated, but the wind was just as wild. In all the excitement with Mary, she had almost forgotten about the storm. She followed him to the door and looked out. He was walking around their car assessing all the damage and probably blowing off steam from her comments. She didn't care. She wasn't backing down. She had learned to stand her ground the last few years. He would have to live with her decision. Her only problem was her poor ability to lie.

She remembered how hard it had been to keep Phil from learning about Jerry's attempt to grope her. She had managed to keep the incident from Phil, but Detective Partridge had seen right through her. He had questioned her in private while investigating Jerry's murder. Now she was afraid she wouldn't be able to keep information about Mary's letter and diaries from the police. They were smarter than Phil when it came to seeing through stories. Her only hope was her obvious shock and near hysteria over Mary's death. Hopefully, she would have enough time to get through the diaries and decide what to do before she was questioned in great detail. Maybe they wouldn't even question her that much. She lifted the box and brought it into her bedroom. She did not want to glance at it by mistake when talking to the police.

And then, from her bedroom, she heard Phil's voice as he opened the front door. She shoved the box into the closet, grabbed some tissues from the bathroom, and ran to see what was going on.

"Judy, this is Officer Rinaldo. He said he got here as soon as he could. He wants to talk to us."

"Thank God you're here," she managed to say while holding back the tears that were forming once more. "We've been waiting for you. Come into the living room, and please sit down. We have a little light in here from our lanterns." She was trying to sound natural. She was trying to keep from crying, so she blurted out a question while sniffling a little. "How's the driving out there? What's going on in town with this storm?"

"To tell you the truth," Rinaldo said while smiling warmly, "the driving is lousy. Trees are down everywhere, and it's hard to drive. Cleanup's going to be a mess. Now, Mrs. Weinberger, I understand you're the one who discovered the body. Must have been awful for you. Are you okay to answer a few questions? I know finding your friend must have been quite a shock. My partner is next door waiting for the medical examiner. I'm sure he's having trouble getting around like the rest of us. Tell me in your own words, if you can, how you discovered the body of your neighbor. Take your time."

She thought she would be able to talk with the police, but she immediately broke down. "I can't believe . . . I can't believe . . . oh my God. Help me Phil. You tell him," and she began to shake and cry all over again.

"Officer Rinaldo," said Phil, "I'll try to fill you in as best I can. Judy, you jump in whenever you feel you can talk." Phil explained, "Well, we heard this big crash, which was that huge tree you see down on our car. Judy was worried about Mary, I mean Mrs. Rafferty. They're good friends. Actually they kind of adopted one another, you know, like mother and daughter. My wife's mother died a few years ago, and Mary has no family. It kind of worked out for both of them."

Judy listened. She did not want to talk to the officer. She was afraid he might ask her something she did not want to answer. She kept telling herself to be strong and act sincere.

"So Judy said she was going to check on Mary to see if she was okay; you know, not spooked by the storm," said Phil. "Well the next thing I know I hear screaming, and Judy comes running out of Mary's house. Judy is white as a ghost, excuse the cliché, but she really looked that awful. She can hardly speak. She's shaking, gagging, crying, and choking. I even shook her to try and calm her down so I could understand what she was saying. She couldn't talk. She drags me into Mary's house and into the bathroom. I felt sick myself when I saw what had happened. I asked if she had touched anything."

"Officer." Judy's tissue was rolled into a ball, and she was kneading it like it was a piece of dough. "Officer," she sniffled and blew her nose. "I only touched the door to the house, the door to the bedroom, and the door to the bathroom. And then I started to scream, and I ran to get Phil."

"Mrs. Weinberger, since you knew Mrs. Rafferty so well, do you have any idea why someone would want to harm her? Did she have any enemies? Did she ever tell you she was afraid of anything?"

There it was, Judy thought, the kind of questioning she wanted to avoid. Okay, she reminded herself, be a big girl. Look him in the eyes and answer no. "No Officer," she said. "Mary never said she was afraid of anything. We usually talked about everyday things. You know—the weather, shopping, television programs, the latest gossip. I don't know. I guess nothing important."

"We'll have to contact the next of kin," said Rinaldo. "Do you have that information Mrs. Weinberger?"

"Officer," Phil answered for her. "As we said, Mary

didn't have any family. She always said she was all alone. We never questioned her, and Judy and I tried to act like family for her. You know, like inviting her over for dinner at times and often including her when our grandkids visited. She loved our little ones and said we were the family she never had."

God bless Phil, Judy thought. She loved him at that moment because she knew she couldn't have answered without sounding evasive. "What will happen to her?" Judy asked. "I mean, what do the police do in a situation like this?" She was trying to act normal although she didn't know what normal was in this situation. "I mean, I've just found the body of a very good friend. A very good friend who felt like a mother to me." And then Judy started to cry and shake again. "I'm sorry," she managed to mumble. "It's too awful. Who would want to kill Mary and why? She was such a nice, caring sweet lady."

"I understand your grief," said Officer Rinaldo. "Please rest assured that we will do everything in our power to get to the bottom of this crime. We're a small town with a small force, and murder is a very infrequent occurrence here. When it happens, we put all our energy into solving it. Other officers will contact you as soon as possible to begin the official investigation. I'm not totally sure, but Detectives Partridge and Cotter usually are the ones to handle this type of crime."

"We know them, don't we Phil," said Judy. "They helped solve the murder of my friend Susan and her husband Jerry. You probably remember the case, officer. It seems like only yesterday that we found out Susan's death wasn't an accident and that her husband Jerry had killed her and made it look like an accident. And now another friend is dead. I can't stand it."

"I remember the case vividly," said Rinaldo. "It had so many wild twists and turns. It caught the imagination of everyone at the station. We even talk about that one occasionally when we do our Citizen's Police Academy Program. And now, if you don't have any other questions for me, I need to get on with my work. This has been an awful night for all of us, and we need to secure the crime scene and get back out to help with the storm. We'll be contacting both of you in the morning for any additional information you might have remembered. Here's my card, and please call the station if you think of anything before we get back to you. Stay safe tonight, and let's pray that you don't get any other damage from the storm."

Phil walked him to the door and mumbled, "Thank you for coming. I know it's hard getting around. How soon do you think they'll be removing Mary from the house? I hate to think of her lying there in the bathtub. It's so awful. My wife is quite upset, as you can see. What kind of a person does something like this? Do you think it was random, or do you think she was targeted?"

"Can't say Mr. Weinberger. It's much too early to form any opinions. We have a lot of work to do here, and we'll have to collect evidence and go from there. We'll be in touch. Take good care of the Mrs. She's in a state of shock. It's not easy seeing what she saw; her being a close friend and all. And now, if you'll excuse me, I need to get back next door."

"Phil, what else did he say?" Judy asked as Phil closed the door. "When will they get back to us?"

"He didn't say anything other than they would be collecting evidence. I bet there's loads of evidence in those diaries. I still think you're obstructing justice. You'd better think long and hard about them in the next few hours. You do realize, I hope, that it's a crime to hide them from the police."

"Not if they don't know about them," said Judy. "You and I are the only ones who know they exist. Are you going to turn me in, your own wife? Don't look at me like that. I'm going to read them first, and then I'll decide what to do. I owe it to Mary."

"Right, you owe it to Mary. I don't think so! You know, sometimes I don't get you. A murder has been committed here, and you're wrong, very wrong."

"We'll see," Judy said. Her plan was to get out of bed as soon as Phil fell asleep that night and start reading the diaries. Maybe there was nothing in them, and then again . . .

CHAPTER 2

After the police left, Judy headed to the den with the box of diaries. She had decided to read now rather than sneak out of bed after Phil fell asleep since there was nothing for her to do anyway but listen to the storm. She had a good lantern, an afghan to wrap around her legs that her grandmother had knit years ago, and the thermos of tea she had made earlier in the day before they lost power. She loved that old afghan. It was warm, and it always felt like Gram was enveloping her. Her grandmother had made it out of old wool remnants, and it always looked rag tag. None of the colors worked together. They had simply been chosen at random and knit into different sized squares, but Judy had always treasured it.

"Phil, did you go upstairs?" she yelled. "I'm in the den with Mary's diaries. I'll call you if I come across anything. Are you still at your desk? You can sit down here with me if you want. It won't disturb me as long as you don't try to bully me."

"Thanks for the invitation," he said sarcastically. "I'm almost finished at my desk, if you must know, and then I'm going to bed where it's warm. And don't bother me unless it's related to the murder. I don't have to be woken up to learn about Mary's life of crime. You can knock yourself out reading."

Judy reached into the box, took out the earliest diary, and began to read . . .

Dear Diary,

I haven't written in a diary for a long time, but somehow it feels like the right thing to do. I used to write in one every day, but I destroyed all of them because I was afraid of what might happen if someone found them. A lot happened in the past, and at my age I think I want to start to remember. I want to try to understand how it affected me and what the past means for my future. I know that sounds crazy, but my whole life has been kind of crazy. Not now though. Now for the first time I've really found a home, a place to live out my life with people who care about me. They don't know anything about me, yet they've accepted me as I presented myself. I've been so many people that sometimes I find it hard to remember all of them. But I need to remember. I think if I remember and write about it, then maybe I can forgive myself. Maybe I can even come to share who I am with Phil and Judy, who treat me like family. I'm not ready to tell them the truth, but I think I'm ready to tell myself the truth. Maybe someday I'll share this diary with them, and then I won't have to struggle for the right words. Maybe I'll ask them to read the diary first, and then sit down with them and talk about my life. That would be crazy, but it would be beautiful to finally stop living a lie and be truly loved for who I am by my new family.

Who am I? Now that's a good question. Am I who I want to be, am I who I should be, am I who others think I am, or am I who others want me to be? Wow, that's a lot of different ways to try to understand myself. Should have done this years ago, but this is the first time I've felt safe enough and loved enough to think about coming clean. I'm coming to the end of my life; well, not literally, I hope. But I'm in my late seventies, and I've already lived the majority of my life. I hope I have many more years ahead of me because my life right now is one of peace, and that is the most wonderful feeling in the world and one that I have searched for my entire life . . .

Judy read the next entry.

Dear Diary,

Here goes . . . the beginning of my story. I was born in a small town in Florida that will remain unnamed for the time being. I don't know how this is going to work, and I don't want this to fall into the wrong hands with innocent people getting into trouble. Not sure why they would, but I need to get this down on paper, and I don't want to take the time to think that part through. So maybe I am a little paranoid. Maybe I have and maybe I haven't a reason to feel that way, but time will tell. Alright, enough of that. Now for my story.

Life in that small town was good, really good. We didn't have a lot of money, but who did then. My father had been in the Navy during the war, the big one, WWII. After the war, we moved to a small house that my father bought under the GI Bill. That bill provided low interest rates to allow returning veterans the opportunity to buy a home. Of course it was also meant to stimulate the economy. There were four of us . . . my mother, my father, my sister, and myself. I was the younger one. My sister was an over-achiever who excelled in high school and at everything she did. She later went to nursing school and became a registered nurse. I was different! I hated school and everything about school. To me, everything we were learning was a waste of time. My parents were always on my case. They would throw my sister up to me as a model of how I should lead my life. They aggravated the hell out of me, and I aggravated the hell out of them.

As soon as I graduated from high school, I split. I left a note saying goodbye. I told my family not to look for me. I didn't want to be found, but of course they found me. I ran away many times, and eventually they stopped trying to bring me back. I was nothing but a problem to them, and my antics took a toll on both my parents. I finally ended up on the streets of Miami. It wasn't that far from my home, but in terms of culture, it was miles away.

I remember my first day and Joey . . .

"Hey there girl. What ya doing?"

That was Mary's first encounter with Joey. Joey was at the bus stop when she arrived in Miami with her light blue suitcase and her beehive hairdo. She thought she looked like a million bucks, and he told her that he did too.

"You're a real looker. Anyone ever tell ya that? If not, they should. Let me guess. You're here meeting ya boyfriend, and he's late. Girl, don't be mad at him. He's probably out buying ya some pretty flowers as a welcome to our town."

Mary knew she shouldn't talk to him. In her head she could hear her mother screaming to beware of strangers. So she turned around and walked in the opposite direction. She didn't know where it lead, and she was afraid of getting lost. Joey could tell what she was doing, and he waited for her to turn back in his direction. Of course she did.

"Not going to kill ya, girl. Just recognize that lost stare when I see it. No one's going to meet ya, huh? Left home for the big city, I bet. Can spot it every time. Tell ya what. Here's my card, Joey Dee, Miami Social Worker. Come by here a few times a week to look around, ya know. Always one of you girls getting off the bus and looken lost. Like I said, can always spot a new girl. So what now, now that ya finally here, here in the promised land? Do ya have a destination, a place to stay? Bet you're playing it by ear.

Don't want to scare ya. Number's on the card if ya want some help. Know some safe motels that won't rip ya off. Maybe might even be able to get ya a job as a chambermaid. Think about it. I'm always around."

He stuck out his hand to shake hers and then gave her his card. Mary glanced at it, put it in her pocket, and thanked him.

"Remember me, girl. I'm available to help twenty-four seven. Try to smile some. Got a real nice smile there."

And then he walked away. After Joey Dee, no one else even glanced at her let alone talked to her. Mary was nervous, but she knew she would be fine because she had a plan. She wanted to be near the water, near the beach. She had lived inland, and the beach had been an infrequent treat. The movie *Beach Party* with Frankie Avalon and Annette Funicello had been a favorite of hers, and she wanted to have fun like they did. She had studied the map and knew she needed to walk east when she got off the bus if she wanted to get to a beach. Her grandmother used to come to Miami every winter from Boston. She never stayed with them because her grandmother and her mother had had an awful fight, at least that was how the story went. Her grandmother never visited them, and they never visited her. But she always sent Mary postcards from Miami. Mary had saved all of them including her last one . . .

**"Hi Sweetheart,
How are you? You must be real big by now. Well, here I am in Miami again. It's good for the bones, you know, away from the Boston winters. If you ever get to Miami in the winter or Boston in the summer, please visit me darling. I really miss seeing you. This is a picture of my motel here in Miami. Nice place. It's cheap and in a safe part of town. Be a good girl and listen to your folks. Love Grammy"**

Mary's grandmother had died a few years earlier, but Mary had that last postcard and the motel was her destination—Silver Sands Motel, 301 Ocean Drive, Miami. She loved the name, it was close to the beach, and that was where she was headed.

"I remember your grandmother," the owner said.

He was a fat guy, the kind whose stomach hangs over his belt. He was bald, too, with a great big brown spot on top of his head, but it was his nose that caught her attention. She had always hated men with dark, bushy protruding nose hairs. That was one thing about her father. He was fastidious about that kind of thing. But this guy — she tried not to stare.

"Real nice lady, your grandmother. She talked about her grandchildren all the time. You kept a post card, and now you're here. Imagine that. Too bad your grandmother's gone. What can I do for you? I'm sure you didn't just come by to say hello."

"Well see . . . " she smiled feeling a little more at ease now that she had found the motel and a guy who he even remembered her grandmother. "I need a place to stay, and I need a job. I left home. I mean I'm old enough to leave. I graduated high school, and I want to try and take care of myself."

"Well young lady, you're in luck. One of my chambermaids up and quit on me yesterday. Following her boyfriend out West or something, so I was going to put out an ad for new help. If you want the job, you can have it. Doesn't pay much, but it comes with a room that has a small fridge and a hot plate. What do you think? Is that what you had in mind or were you hoping for something, you know, a little more professional? That I can't help you with, sorry."

She jumped at the opportunity, thanked him over and

over again as if he had just given her a hundred dollar bill, and promised she would do a good job. His name was Dominic, and he told her she could begin the next day.

"This is your room, honey," he said while blowing his nose. "It's next to the laundry. Machines make a racquet, so I can't rent the room out, know what I mean. But you'll get used to the noise. How about twenty dollars a week for a salary? That includes your room, which, of course, is no charge. Use it myself when I'm too tired to drive home. But, knew your grandmother and need someone pronto. Besides, you seem like a sweet kid. You can even stay in the room tonight if you need a place to stay right away. What do you say? Do we have a deal?"

Mary thanked him again and couldn't stop grinning. She had her own room and a job, and she had only come off the bus an hour earlier.

After a week into her new job, she was still smiling. The work was manageable, and she loved the fresh smell of the rooms after they were cleaned. Cecelia, the other chambermaid, showed Mary the ropes and entertained her with stories about the guests and about Dominic. Cecelia said she and Dominic were an item, and his wife didn't know anything because they were very careful.

"You better stay away from him or I cut you!" she screamed at Mary after a few weeks. "I see him staring at you. He's mine, so you stay away!"

Cecelia's threats frightened Mary. She certainly wasn't interested in Dominic. Who would be she thought. Cecelia could have him, with his fat stomach falling over his pants and his awful nose. She had little money and spent nearly every cent she earned on food and other necessities. She kept to herself and rarely ventured from the property other than to sit at the beach and read. And then it happened.

Dominic called her into his office. "We have a big problem here, and I need an explanation!" he screamed.

"Some guests have complained of missing items in their rooms and guess what . . . they happen to be the rooms you clean. I was shocked to think that you would steal from my guests, and I had to check it out. So I went to your room and surprise, surprise. I found a box shoved under your bed with some of the missing items. I want an explanation, dammit, and I want it right now young lady!"

"I don't have one," she stammered shocked by the accusation. "Why would I? I haven't done anything."

Dominic glared at her and said, "I'm sorry. This is a very small motel, and I can't afford bad publicity. Please remove your things right now and give me all your keys. You certainly are nothing like your grandmother. She was a fine, respectable woman. You should be ashamed of yourself. She must be turning over in her grave right now."

Mary was devastated and told him so. Despite her tears, her insistence that she hadn't touched anything, and her plea for a chance to prove her innocence, she found herself on the street.

With no place to stay and with no job, she began to wander the streets. Going home was not an option. She thought her job had been going well, and then she thought of Cecelia's threat and wondered if Cecelia had taken the items and put them in Mary's room to get her fired. Mary never paid attention to Dominic, but he hung around her all the time. He complimented her on her job and said he might give her more responsibility if she kept up the good work. She became excited and worked even harder. That was when Cecelia had stopped being friendly and screamed at her to stay away from Dominic. That bitch, Mary thought, but there was no way to prove her innocence.

Now back on the street, Mary remembered Joey Dee's words that he would be available to help twenty-four seven. She reached into her jacket pocket, the one she had worn when she arrived on the bus, and found his business card.

She stared at the number and thought about her options. She did not have any. She had wandered all day long, she was hungry, and she had no place to stay. Cecelia had cheated her out of her last week's pay, and now she was afraid to spend the little money she had. She decided to call Joey Dee. The card said he was a social worker, and he had seemed nice. Maybe he could help.

Joey met her at a nearby diner, treated her to dinner, and explained how he could solve her problem. "I know a house where girls live til they get independent. Ya know, til they get on their feet with a job and money for their own place. Some girls even become friends and move in together. What do ya think? You can come and check it out if ya want." He reached out to hold her hand and told her not to cry. "I know Miami, and I know the streets. I can help ya if ya want."

They sat around and talked for over an hour. She told him about herself, her family life, and her hopes for the future. "Joey, you're so easy to talk to," she said. "I can't believe I was afraid of you when I arrived in town a few weeks ago. I need your help."

He drove her to the house he had described. It was in a run-down section of town, but he explained that Miami rents were high and his girls were not fussy. A few days later she had a new job at the motel across the street. It was not near the beach; it was not the greatest looking place; the guests were not the best, but it was a job. She promised herself that she would move and find a better job once she saved enough money. After her first week on the job, Joey came to visit.

"Hi there Mary. How's life going?" Joey said. "Any problem with the girls? Any complaint about the guests? I know ya not happy here. I know ya feel like ya can do better, that ya come from much better, but run away from home, and it's what ya get. Now I helped a lot, but gotta make money ya know," and he smiled at her.

Mary began to feel uncomfortable. She thought Joey was simply some guy who befriended her because there are nice people out there. He had told her he was a social worker, and she had trusted him.

"So," Joey said now smirking at her, "need to recoup my money. Bought ya dinner and drove ya here. Gas costs money ya know. And, of course, my time. I don't come cheap. This here's Miami, babe, the big city. I need to live too! Here's the deal. Ya give me ya pay the next two weeks; we call it square."

"Joey, I won't have any money. I spent everything I took from home getting myself here, and I have to eat. The rent at the place you took me isn't much, but I need to pay for that. I can't give you my whole paycheck. How about a little each week? I could do that. I thought you were a social worker. I thought you help people."

"I am a social worker, honey. I work for Joey, doing social work, like being friendly to all the girls pouring into town looking for fun, independence, and money. So sorry darlin, can't help ya. Got bills to pay, and so do you. Be by on Friday, and ya better cough up the paycheck if ya know what's good for ya. What'd ya think the deal was when ya left home? Did ya think it would be a free ride with the streets supporting ya while ya played grown up? Don't work that way. Friday, and better not disappoint." He grinned this time and left her standing there close to tears.

Mary ran to her room and threw herself on the bed. She was frantic. What could she do? How would she live? Going home was not an option. So she stood up, gazed into the mirror, and said, "You're a survivor, and you'll do whatever it takes. You'll get through this." Then she washed her face and walked across the street to her job.

The guy caught her going through his clothes. She thought his room was empty. She had knocked, and when there was no answer, she had gone in to clean—standard procedure. How could she know he was in the bathroom. She saw a pair of men's pants on the bed with a few dollar bills sticking out of the pocket. She thought no one would miss a few bucks, and she needed every dollar she could get. So she closed the door, reached into the pocket, grabbed a five, and quickly stuck it in her bra. She turned to reopen the door. They were required to keep the door open while cleaning a room—policy the boss had told her. When she glanced up, she saw a guy standing in front of her.

"Hey, what do you think you're doing? That's my money. Hand it over."

"I'm sorry. I don't know what I was thinking. I saw the money and thought you wouldn't miss a few dollars. I need money, and it was just there. I didn't plan it. Look, I've never done anything like this before. Please don't tell anyone. I don't want to lose this job. Please mister. I'll do an extra special job cleaning your room to make it up to you. Please." She began to shake.

"Tell you what," and he smiled revealing a missing tooth as well as a mouth full of teeth that looked like they had never seen a dentist. "I keep quiet, you keep quiet, you keep the money, and I throw in an extra dollar. What do you say?" and he reached for her chest.

"What are you doing?" she yelled as she lurched back with her hands in the air trying to protect herself. "You can't do that. I'll report you to my boss and to the police!"

He laughed. "And I'll have to report you to your boss as well as the police. Sorry girlie. Give it up. What did you think was going to happen if you got caught? Did you expect maybe a slap on the wrist with a be a good girl now pat on the shoulder? Grow up. You did it; now stand still and pay up."

He grabbed his money and threw her on the bed. "I bet you're even fresh meat! My lucky day. Now shut up, or I'll have to hit you."

It was awful, and he slapped her when she started to scream. When he was through, he put on his pants, grabbed his bag, and threw the five back on the bed with an extra one dollar bill.

"What a place," he said as he grinned from ear to ear. "A clean bed, a good night's sleep, a place to take a dump, and then a surprise waiting for me when I get out . . . a real live girlie with fresh meat. Bye, bye!" And he walked out the door.

She shook as she wiped away her tears. Her underpants and bra lay on the floor, and she was trapped. If she accused him, he would say he caught her trying to steal his money. She stumbled into the bathroom and looked in the mirror. Her hair was a mess, her lip was bleeding, and she had bruises on her arm from where he held her down.

What had she expected? Joey was right—this was for real and she needed to deal with it. So she pulled herself together, washed her face, and cleaned the room. Mary was determined to succeed. She had to. She had run away too many times to fall apart like a big baby the first time she ran into trouble.

Judy stopped reading and put the diary down. She had been sitting in one spot for a long time and needed to stretch. She went into the kitchen to brew some coffee and mumbled . . . "Dummy, you can't make coffee. There's no power." She walked to the front door and looked out. Yellow crime scene tape was draped across Mary's driveway and a police cruiser was parked across the street. Judy needed to finish the diaries as soon as possible. She returned to the den, wrapped herself in the afghan, and continued to read.

"Are you still reading those diaries?" Phil mumbled.

She hadn't heard him come into the den.

"What time is it anyway?" he said. "Are you going to stay up all night reading?"

"Phil, she ran away from home right after high-school, and she was raped, and she couldn't do anything about it because the guy found her trying to steal money from his pocket while she was a chambermaid at some motel in Miami." Judy couldn't get the words out fast enough. "Phil, let me read this to you. It's unbelievable."

"You read about it. Tell me later. I'm going back to bed. It's freezing. Do we have another blanket?"

"How long have you lived here?" Judy snapped. "Check the upstairs linen closet on the third shelf. What's wrong with you? It's not that cold. For God's sake—you're wearing a hat, a sweatshirt, sweatpants, and you already have two blankets. That's a bit much, don't you think?"

"So Miss Smarty Pants, now you know how I feel and how I should feel. It's amazing how smart you are. Why don't you keep your comments to yourself. I know how I feel, and you don't!" And he stormed up the stairs to get an extra blanket.

Judy groaned, exasperated that the smallest things could set him off. She was cold too, but Phil was ridiculous. She wondered if it was his age. He was older, so maybe this was the beginning of a man's old age nonsense. Many retired people lived on the Cape, and she occasionally saw a wife struggling when she and Phil were out and about. She always felt badly when she saw the wife tip-toeing around her husband. The wife would try to be careful about what she said and how she said it, and then the husband would jump down her throat. It was embarrassing to watch, and Judy thought she would die if that happened to them. *You're out of here* was a phrase they used when they were first retired. If you get fat, you're out of here. If you get a face lift, you're out of here. If you spend your life watching sports on television with a beer in your hand, you're out of here. It had been fun to comment about behaviors they hated. But what if Phil exhibited those awful behaviors. She shuddered. She knew she would have to live with him and his actions. You're out of here would never be an option. She shook her head to dismiss her ugly thoughts and went back to the next entry in the diary . . .

Dear Diary,

I remember those days in Miami like it was yesterday. I stayed on at the motel for a while longer, but I learned to do more than clean. I learned how not to get caught while stealing money and stealing anything that could be pawned. It was scary how easy it was if you knew what you were doing, and Joey and his girls knew what they were doing. They taught me everything, and I was a fast learner.

Before I knew it, I had paid off Joey. He said he was proud of me . . .

"Darlin, I think ya ready to move out of this dumpy motel into something better. I've a friend at one of the fancy hotels. Sometimes he hires my girls. Of course, that's if ya interested. You could stay here if ya wanted to, but I think ya destined for bigger things. Could tell the minute ya got off that bus that ya got class. That's something a lot of the girls will never have. They belong in dumps like this. You can go far if ya stick with me. What do ya say?"

"I don't know Joey," she said. "I was really scared when I began to lift stuff to pay you back. I guess I'm not as scared now. I guess it's kind of fun. And the girls have been nice to me, at least most of them. Tell me more."

"Well," he said while grinning from ear to ear, "had this plan for a while, but never found the right girl til now. I think you're the right girl. Ya got looks, ya got smarts, and ya got guts. We could work together like partners. You keep on doing what ya do, but I put ya into one of them fancy places. They have real good pickins, not crap and chump change like ya get here. I mean big stuff. Those New York and Boston people, ya know the rich ones who come down here to get away from the snow, those guys have what we want. And then there's the famous people. Think about it, but don't wait too long cause there's girls coming off those buses all the time. Might find a smart one like ya on the next bus, and then ya'll have blown your big chance."

"Where's that fancy hotel? I mean from here I just walk across Dixie Highway and I'm at work. I don't see any nice hotels around here. How would I get to work?" She was interested, but hesitant. She hadn't been caught stealing, but she knew it was just a matter of time. Maybe she needed to move on. Joey was mean at times, but he had shown her the way. She wondered if she should trust him again.

"My car, of course," he said while smiling at her. "I drive ya to work every day and pick ya up. Remember, partners. Ya get to see how the better half lives, and ya make more money. I can call my friend today and see if he can use ya. Then ya can leave that dumpy motel. Things get good, maybe we can find ya a better place to live. Who knows, but first things first. Let's see if I can get ya that other job."

Joey was true to his word. In a short time she was working at the Eden Roc, and she was impressed. Famous people like Milton Berle, Johnnie Ray, and Nat King Cole were often guests there while they entertained in the hotel's nightclub. They had wives with them, they had girlfriends with them, and they threw money around like it was going out of style. Mary felt guilty whenever she stole a small pieces of jewelry or a few dollars from a guest who left her, the chambermaid, a nice tip. A few were cheap, and they were the ones she enjoyed ripping off. She was careful, and she was always polite when she saw guests in the hallways. She would smile and nod, not like a couple of girls who got fired because they were always asking the famous ones for autographs. She didn't bother anyone. The head of housekeeping gave her good reviews, and he even told her there might be some room for advancement if she kept up the good work.

"Room for advancement means entertaining them," said Joey. "Ya moving fast, moving fast. Knew it when I found ya. We need to hurry and get ya some decent clothes. Ya need to be ready to move when ya get the call. I know Richards. If he alerts a girl to the chance for advancement, it means advancement is on its way real soon. Here's some money. When ya get off, go see Vera up on Lincoln at *The Boutique of Miami*. Tell her Joey sent ya. She'll know how to fix ya up. Do everything she says."

Mary stared into the mirror. She couldn't believe what she saw. Her hair had been cut short, she had been shown how to put on makeup, and she had been fitted for several outfits—casual ones and more formal ones. She wanted to pinch herself. It didn't feel real. She looked and felt like a totally different person. Joey said he would keep everything in his apartment, and he would pick up the clothes that were being altered. This was what she had dreamt about when she ran away from home, and now it was happening.

When Joey dropped her back at the rooming house, she gave him a little hug and said, "Thank you for everything. Thank you. I'm so excited. When do you think Mr. Richards will need me?"

She was moved out of housekeeping and soon became one of Richard's top girls. His special customers loved her, and they were generous tippers. She had repeat business all the time as well as recommendations from satisfied customers. Money was flowing, and she shared it all with Joey.

"See, didn't I tell ya," and he laughed while grinning from ear to ear. He could hardly contain himself. "Ya stuck with me, and now we're both rolling in the dough. But I've got to get ya a decent place to stay. Can't have the star of the Eden Roc escort service living in a dump. You're gonna double my share of the money cause I'm gonna find ya a real nice place to live. Might even move in with ya myself. Ya know, as protection. This is a pretty wild town what with ya coming in late at night. Yup, think ya might need protection."

"I don't know, Joey. I've never lived with a guy before. I'm not that kind of girl," and she coyly smiled at him.

"For not being that kind a girl, ya certainly learned pretty fast. Those guys aren't giving ya all those gifts and all those big tips because ya look pretty sitting next to them at some ritzy restaurant. Tell me, what's ya specialty? Is it sucking cock or maybe ya learned how to play some of those naughty games! Should cut myself into that action."

"I do what they tell me to do. Some of it's gross, but most of it's okay. Remember, you told me to grow up. Well Joey, I'm all grown up. I've learned how to survive, and I've learned I'm pretty good at what I do. It's better than the stealing you had me do. That scared the shit out of me, but I guess I was good, and I was lucky."

"Luck had nothing to do with it girl. You were trained by the best. My girls don't get caught if they're smart and listen to me. You're my top girl now, and the sky's the limit. I told ya I had big plans. This is just the start."

Dear Diary,

Joey told me he had big plans, and I was loving it. Big plans were right up my alley. I left home because I had big plans for my life. I thought I had found them in Miami, but after a while it became routine. At first it had been fun going out every night with a different guy, going to fancy restaurants, and going to great parties. Most of the men were happy if I simply acted like their girlfriends, paid attention to them, and listened to their stories. But sometimes the payback after the fun wasn't so great. Sometimes I'd have clients with strange tastes. I always did what they asked, but some of it was gross.

Joey found us a beautiful place right on the beach. We could look out the front windows and see the Atlantic Ocean and out the back and see the Intercoastal. It was like a dream. I worked hard, sometimes six or seven days in a row. Joey found some books on being an escort, and I studied them to learn new tricks for my customers . . .

Joey smiled his usual smile and said, "We have to keep ya techniques new and fresh if we're gonna keep getting big money. I don't want new girls pushing ya out."

Mary always listened to him even though most of her clients asked for the basics. That was fine with her. She would arrive on a date in expensive casual clothes while carrying a large designer bag filled with goodies including bras, panties, and a garter belt. Joey made her buy everything in either red or black.

"And don't forget those new high heels that I bought ya," he yelled from the other room. "Guys like to see girls in heels wearing a man's white shirt with their panties showing. And remember, roll up the sleeves, and don't wear a bra under the shirt. And for Christ's sake" he screamed, "strut around like I showed ya. I know your date tonight, and that'll really turn him on."

"Don't scream at me. I hate when you scream." She was almost crying. "You aren't my father and you aren't my mother. You're always telling me what to do. I bring in all the money around here. I know you do everything for me, for us, but I'm not a child anymore. I know what I'm doing. I'm not stupid. Don't I keep getting these dates? You aren't with me when I'm working, so stop telling me what to do!"

"Who do ya think ya talking to?" And he spun her around. "I made ya who you are. You were nothing but a scared shitty little kid from the sticks. I taught ya everything. Ya nothing without me. Ya do what I say, when I say it, and how I say it. Ya my cash cow, and now that I'm living in the style in which I was meant to live, I'm not gonna let you dictate how we do things. Understand?" When he let go of her arm, she was left with a large red welt.

Dear Diary,

Joey had frightened me. I hoped I hadn't made a big mistake going back to him. But I had no choices, no options. I had created this life, and it looked like I was never going to break away . . .

Judy stood up and stretched. She had been sitting in one position for a long time, and her right hip was burning. The exercises the physical therapist recommended were keeping her busy, but she wasn't sure they were helping, especially tonight. She had read somewhere that pain like hers was not associated with bad weather, but what did they know. All she knew was when it rained, or when rain was threatened, her hip responded. And with tonight's storm, it was talking loud and clear.

Judy was in total disbelief as she read about Mary's life. She wondered how long Mary had lived with Joey and how long she had been an escort. Mary didn't even remotely seem like she could have been that kind of person. Judy wanted to share the information with someone, but she knew she couldn't share it with anyone but Phil.

She walked to the bedroom and opened the door, hoping Phil was up and in a better mood. She wouldn't wake him, but if he was tossing and turning, she could act like she thought he was awake. She moved near the bed, eager for him to sense that someone was there. It worked. He opened his eyes.

"Oh good. You're up. Phil, you've got to listen to some of what I'm reading about Mary. She was a high paid escort in Miami. Can you believe it?"

"You woke me up to tell me your Mary, your mother figure, was a prostitute. That's a good one." and he laughed.

"I didn't say prostitute. Don't be mean," said Judy. "She had her reasons, and you'd understand her better if you read what I'm reading."

"I don't have to understand her better. I always knew there was something fishy about her. The only ones who need to understand her better are the police, and you better be finished with your reading and ready to turn everything over to them when they question you again. I mean it Judy. If you don't tell them what you have, I will. Now leave me alone and don't wake me again. It's freezing in here." And he turned and rolled up into a ball to try and keep warm.

Judy knew Phil was right. She had to finish the diaries, but she wished he was more interested in what they revealed about Mary. She closed the bedroom door, grabbed her ski hat and gloves from the hall closet, and sat down to read. "Damn," she said, "it's cold in this house." She was glad she hadn't packed away all their ski clothes. Their cold attic was the last place she wanted to visit.

Dear Diary,

We stayed in Miami for several years. The money was good, and there was an unending supply of men who needed a date. I developed a reputation for providing sophisticated companionship with unending fun. Joey made a few contacts for me, but I was the one who brought in all the money and did all the work. He became lazy and ate up a good portion of the money by indulging in his new expensive tastes. I was now his only girl, although we never discussed his business arrangements. I sometimes thought of life without him, but I was afraid. I knew I was leading a dangerous life and Joey would always be there for me. So I put up with his shit. He meant well, at least I thought he meant well . . .

"Hey Mary, I think we're going to leave Miami to travel and see the world. We've got the dough, and I think we're destined for bigger things. Hear there's good pickings across that big ocean. There's Paris, Rome, or even Amsterdam. Hell, Amsterdam. That would be a great city for us. We could set up shop anywhere, and you could do several guys a day for more money than ya make now as an escort. Yup, the more I think about it, the more I think that's the way to go."

Joey was so excited at the prospect of finally traveling out of the country he was practically dancing across the floor. He had always dreamt of traveling to Europe, but he had always felt the dream was out of reach. But now he had Mary, and Mary's ability to bring in the money appeared to have no limits. She was busy every night, and she was bringing in serious money. He had taught her everything she knew, so he felt she owed him.

"Leave Miami? Leave this country? I don't know Joey. We've a good thing going here. It's pretty safe. I have repeat clients, and they pay well. I want to stay here. The thought of going to another country scares me. I wouldn't be able to speak the language. How would that work?"

Joey could tell she was upset when she put down her

glass of wine to crack the knuckles on both her hands. It was a habit Joey tried to break in Mary ever since he first met her. She did it when she was scared, when she was nervous, and when she was upset. "Quit cracking those damn knuckles for Christ's sake. How many times do I have to tell ya? Stop! If guys see ya, they'll think you're nothing but a scared little kid, and they won't pay the high prices we're used to getting. So stop, damnit!

"We'll go to Amsterdam. They speak English, so ya won't have to worry. And there's loads of tourists there who'll pay good money to spend time with ya. We'll set up shop; it's legal there. We stick ya in a window, and we're open for business. None of this playing around with one date a night. I want more money and less fancy gifts and fancy dinners like ya keep getting. So it's settled. Pack the bags cause we're going to Amsterdam!"

Mary began to cry. "You can't be serious. I'm not going. I'm happy here. I understand how business works in this country, and I don't want to leave. It frightens me." And she stamped her foot like a young child, crossed her arms, and said, "I'm not going, and that's the end of that."

"Who the hell do ya think you are!" Joey screamed and calmly walked over and slapped her across the face. "Don't ya ever raise a voice to me, and don't ya ever tell me what ya will or won't do. I say what ya will or won't do. I own ya baby. I made ya, and don't ya forget it. If I didn't take ya under my wing and lead the way, ya'd have been dead on the street in no time, or ya'd have gone crawling back home. So remember who ya talking to. We've got the money, and we're going. If ya try any funny stuff, ya'll be sorry!"

Joey was an expert at using women to make a buck, and Mary had become his best moneymaker. He had learned his trade on the streets and used his charm to win them over. He was a long way from the bullied skinny kid who always came home crying. His mother would laugh and tell him to toughen up. She taught him how to survive on the streets. And now, thanks to Mary, he was surviving and thriving beyond his wildest expectations. So Joey certainly had no intention of letting her leave him or dictate their relationship.

Dear Diary,

We went to Amsterdam like Joey wanted. It was then that I realized what my relationship with Joey was all about. He ruled everything in my life—he ruled me. I had no choice because I was afraid to be on my own. I was afraid to run away. I should have left him in Miami. I wondered if this was my new life, a prisoner of Joey's whims? Life in Amsterdam was strange. I couldn't believe what I was doing was perfectly legal. Joey told me he had learned all about Amsterdam's sex business from a guy in Miami . . .

"That's right, ya heard me," he had said. "It's legal in Amsterdam because they know men need their thrills. That way the government controls everything and protects the girls. A girl can rent a room in a special part of town called the Red Light District, charge guys, and the police won't arrest them. And the money is good, real good." Joey was practically drooling when he told her about Amsterdam's policy.

And now it had been a couple of years, and she was one of the regulars. She had wanted to do some sightseeing when they first arrived, but Joey was insistent.

"Start work immediately, and then maybe we talk about sightseeing after the money begins to roll in. What we had going in Miami was chump change compared to the potential here. And besides, ya were getting too friendly with some of those guys. Christ, that Harold guy or

51

whatever the hell his name was, kept calling ya to keep him company. There's no money in keeping guys company. I told ya that we don't make money when ya get paid by going to nice restaurants and getting nice presents. We make money when strangers pay ya cash for a few minutes like they do here and then they go bye-bye and the next guy comes in."

And so Mary went to work every day. She sat at a window dressed in fancy underwear and smiled as men passed, hoping to get one to stop. When she got a man to show interest, she would negotiate a price based on what he wanted. There was always an endless stream of men passing by because Amsterdam was a tourist town, and for tourists, sex out in the open was a novelty. She worked most days from noontime until after midnight. The days were long and boring if she had no customers. During those down times, she liked to read.

"Joey, how about I just work during the day sometimes and sometimes just in the evening? The girls told me we can rent a room for a day or for a night. They said we don't have to rent it by the month. What do you say? Sometimes I get so tired. Then maybe we could do a little sightseeing. I've been here for a long time, and I never go anywhere. I don't know anything about Amsterdam beyond these streets and our little apartment. I'd love to take a boat ride down one of the canals and have lunch at one of the outside cafes. What do you say? Please Joey. You know how hard I work, and I do everything you tell me to do. Please. Please say yes."

"Ya shittin me, right?" and he grabbed her by the arm until she let out a yelp. "How long do ya think ya gonna pull in that kind of money? These are ya best years. Another few, and maybe we can talk. For now, ya keep on working," and he glared at her before walking out of the room.

Mary began to cry. Her life was a mess, and she didn't know what to do. She was stuck in the sex capitol of the world, Amsterdam, with only a high school education and the skills of a prostitute. She needed to get away from Joey, so she decided to discuss her dilemma with one of the girls. Joey didn't know she had made some friends.

Her favorite, a woman named Jennie, was much older than Mary. Jennie was the one who taught her how business was conducted in the district. At first Mary listened to Joey, but she soon discovered he didn't know everything. Jennie knew everything. She had been in the district forever, and everyone admired her. "Don't give him all your money," she said to Mary. "He doesn't have to know what you make. Sneak a little bit at a time for yourself. You never know when you might need it. Not much, you know, you don't want him to become suspicious. You're lucky. You're one of the successful girls. Don't know how you do all those hours day after day. Girl, you're going to burn yourself out. You need to take care. Don't know if you realize it, but not many girls have a guy around their neck. We work for ourselves. But you, you're different. That Joey guy of yours is a beast. He should try this work; bet he wouldn't last long. Can you see him trying to walk after working here for a week. Bet he'd be crawling," and they both laughed.

Mary loved talking to Jennie. She was Mary's only real friend. The other girls were jealous of Mary because she had the most customers. Joey had talked her into dressing as an American school girl with pigtails, and men loved the novelty. Many were European. To them, Mary was fresh and unique. Business was good—too good for Mary, but Joey loved it.

"I'm thinking I might get me another girl," he casually said one night. "Ya know, to bring in even more money. I understand the ropes now, so I'll train her. Then ya can give her some of ya special tips. I know ya talk to that Jennie woman all the time. She's one of the ancient ones, so I bet she's taught ya a few good tricks. Yup, that's what I'm gonna do. Ever see young ones nosing around, send them to me. I'll fix them up real good. No accident ya the busiest window on the street."

Mary didn't say a word. Why would any girl want a guy like Joey, she thought. Most girls worked for themselves. All the money they earned belonged to them. That was the beauty of the *Red Light District*. Every time Mary thought about her situation, she wanted to scream. It wasn't bad enough that she had stupidly run away from home. It wasn't bad enough that she had become mixed up with Joey. No, she had to make her situation even worse. She had to leave the country with him. Mary discussed her mess with Jennie.

"Don't cry about the past," Jennie said. "Plan your future. If you don't like this life, do something about it. Complaining will get you no place. Me, I'm different. First of all, I'm my own boss. And that makes a big difference. I can't imagine my life with the likes of your Joey. I know he doesn't harm you or anything, at least that's what I hear you telling me. But to work as hard as you do, and then to turn the money over to him—that's a crime. And now he wants your help to find another girl. How dumb does he think you are? We have to get you out of here. Me, I'm too old to leave this business. It's the only thing I know. But you, you're still young. And although you got yourself into this mess, I don't think you're stupid. I think you were naïve. Let me think about your problem and how to resolve it. I know all kinds of people. We'll figure it out. Now wipe your face and put on some fresh makeup. The afternoon tourists are on their way."

"I love you Jennie," Mary said. "You're like a big sister," and she gave Jennie a huge hug.

"And I love you too. But you're just a kid, and I've been at this a long time. Don't give up hope. You'll get through it and even laugh about it someday."

Dear Diary,

I continued life in the Amsterdam window until I met this wonderful man. I thought he was a client. I was in the window as usual wearing my bikini underwear with my hair tied in pigtails trying to assume the innocent look of a typical American schoolgirl, whatever that was. Joey made me practice for hours when we first arrived in Amsterdam until he felt I had the American schoolgirl act down pat. When he was satisfied, he said I was ready for tourists who like that sort of thing. So there I was that day trying to attract someone's attention when I noticed this older couple. They were walking slowly, and they were holding hands. They appeared to be glancing at each window, whispering to one another for a few minutes, and then continuing on. As they got closer to my window, I was drawn to look at them. They both smiled at me, and I smiled back. I watched as they spoke to one another. The man shook his head, hesitated, and then came to my door. I was amazed. Why had he stopped at my door after passing so many others? I opened the door, and he asked me my price. After a momentary glance at the woman, he entered. I pulled the curtain closed and started to undress . . .

"Please don't undress," he said somewhat nervously. He was an older gentleman, perhaps in his early sixties. "I only want to talk to you. I know this will sound crazy, but my wife and I, the lady you saw me with, well we lost our daughter to prostitution almost a year ago. We have never recovered from her death, and we think about her every day. We came up with this crazy idea. Well, actually my wife did. She said if we try to take a girl out of prostitution who reminds us of our daughter, maybe we can heal a little bit. I told her she was nuts, but I gave in. I'll do anything to take her out of her awful depression. See we're Americans, and you reminded us of our daughter Amy. I know it's none of my business, but my wife wanted me to ask if you were here against your wishes. She wanted you to know we could help."

Mary was shocked. She had been talking to Jennie for weeks about how to escape from Joey. Then this stranger walks up to her window and offers to help. What if Joey suspected something and set this up as a trap. She immediately became suspicious.

"Please don't be afraid," he said. "I know what you're probably thinking. You probably think this is a scam. Trust me, it's not. If you want, I'll leave now, and you'll never see me or my wife again. I told her it was a crazy idea. But I love her, and if this could relieve some of our pain—some of her pain—I'm willing to try. Take my card, and if you're interested in our help, we're staying at the *Amsterdam Prinsengrach*. We'll be there until next week, and then we fly back to the states. You could come with us, or we could get you a ticket, and you could fly back by yourself. You see, money is not a concern. Financially we've been very successful, but all the money in the world doesn't help us in our sorrow. Perhaps, if we help someone like you, we can find a bit of peace." . . .

Dear Diary,

That man saved my life. At first I was hesitant. I took his card, and he left. I told Jennie about it the next day. She agreed it was hard to believe, but she thought I should try and find out something about the man and his wife. I called their hotel and found that they were in fact guests there. So I told Joey I wanted to bring a book to work like some of the other girls who read when the street is quiet. He wasn't happy, but a few days later he dropped me off at the Tropenmuseum, a grand early 20th-century building that has a museum and library. I asked the librarian to help me check past issues of American newspapers for a story about the man's daughter. I told the librarian I was a friend. Well the story was true. I found an extensive article in one of the papers and learned that they were prominent people in the city. So I called them at their hotel the next day, and we formulated a plan . . .

"Joey, I need a few dollars to buy new clothes for work. Mine are getting worn out from washing. I haven't been as busy as usual, and I think it's because I'm losing that fresh American girl look. How about I go shopping before work?"

"Christ, ya know I have an appointment to check out a car this morning. I don't have time for you. Not a lot of cars around here what with all those damn bikes, but I'll show them how Americans live. I'm getting rid of that heap I bought when we first got here. Wait til they see this new car. Then I'll really have respect on the street. Girls will be clamoring to work for me."

"Please Joey. I can take the tram from here to the *Dappermarkt*. Jennie told me it's not too far away, and people buy everything there from underwear for a dollar, to shampoo, fruit, and even flowers. I can buy some new clothes and then walk to work. You can show me the new car when you pick me up later." She tried to sound casual as she smiled at Joey.

"Don't be stupid! I'm only looking at the car. Ya can't get a car here in a day. Don't ya know anything? Think I want a silver one. Yup, a big shiny silver Cadillac. That'll show them who's king on the street. Then, with another girl, well the sky's the limit. Pick ya up at 2 a.m. as usual. Wait til they see it. They'll know whose gonna own the street soon. Here's a couple bucks. If it's cheap, I want change."

Dear Diary,

As soon as he left, I knew what to do. I knew where he kept the money. I had seen him hide it a million times. And now I needed it, all of it. He liked to see his money, my hard-earned money, so he never brought it to a bank. He said he didn't trust the damn banks. There was plenty there. We lived frugally because he was saving money for his damn car, saving to rent more windows, and saving to move out of our dump some day. We sure lived in a dump. It was a walkup on Bloedstraatthat Street. Our apartment faced the back of a restaurant where they dumped all the garbage. Joey hated the flies and the odor, but he wouldn't move. Said he didn't want to draw attention to himself. I thought that silver Cadillac sure sounded like a bad idea for someone who didn't want to draw attention to himself. I took all the money. I was afraid to count it, so I just threw it all in my bag. Jennie had convinced me to trust the couple because I had no other options. I was to meet them at their hotel that afternoon for an evening flight to the states. He had hidden my passport with all the money, so I had that too along with my few belongings. I quickly left the apartment. They were waiting for me at their hotel as they had promised. I kept thinking ... this flight to the states and then I'll be back on American soil and away from Joey. I wondered what away from Joey meant. I was twenty-six years old with no skills and no contact with my family. How could I go back and face them? How would I support myself? Those questions were foremost in my mind as I flew over the Atlantic and away from my life in an Amsterdam window . . .

Judy and Phil had visited Amsterdam last fall, and

Judy was in disbelief when she read that Mary had lived there. Judy always discussed everything with Mary, yet Mary never said a word about Amsterdam. The two of them had even plotted on ways to coerce Phil into taking the trip. Of course, Judy had begged Phil for a month before he agreed to go. Since their retirement, Judy had successfully pushed him to visit Paris, London, and Rome—all the big tourist spots. They had not traveled while they were working and raising their family. Phil was the practical one. He always promised they would travel when the kids were out of the house, and they no longer had the same money obligations. He liked to aggravate her and say travel is a waste of money because the experience is over in a flash and then you have nothing to show for the money you spent.

As Judy thought about her conversations with Mary, she wondered if she had missed something. When she and Phil returned home from their trip, Judy showed Mary their pictures, and discussed everything—the museums, the canals, the coffee shops that sold marijuana, the food, everything. Even with all that information, Mary never acknowledged that she had lived in or even visited Amsterdam. Judy thought she knew Mary, but now she was beginning to wonder who this women was that lived next door to them. Phil always told Judy there was something odd about Mary's story. Judy hated when Phil was right. She told herself there had to be a reason for Mary's secrecy. Judy knew she had to keep reading.

CHAPTER 3

Police Chief Yablonski glanced around the station and shook his head. Other than the two dispatchers and himself, there was no one else in the station. "That was one hell of a night. Do you have the report?" he asked O'Malley, one of the dispatchers.

"What a mess," agreed O'Malley. "Good thing we had enough of a warning for our town departments to prepare. Cotter was damn lucky he didn't get killed. Heard the tree just missed him but did a number on the car. He's with Partridge now. They're over at Northridge investigating that murder as if we didn't have enough on our plate. Other than the murder, Chief, there were no reported deaths or injuries related to the storm. We do have reports of over forty sizeable trees down and about eight roads blocked, including this end of Route 151. We're clearing all major roads now for emergency vehicle access. We fielded about five-hundred calls yesterday and responded to seventy-two, including the murder. We've officers on 151 directing traffic where the lights are down, as well as at all major detours. We may need to put someone on at the gas stations if lines there get to be a problem. Just got a couple of calls about a fight because someone tried to break into one of those lines. I don't know what the rush for gas is all about with all the blocked roads in town. And also, Chief, there's only a handful of people left over at the high-school shelter. We serviced about seventy-five over there, including five dogs and a cat".

"Awful storm, just awful," said Yablonski while picking at his nails.

What is with him, thought O'Malley, as he watched Yablonski stick a finger in his mouth to bite at a nail. A grown guy, and he was always playing with his damn fingernails. Everyone at the station told jokes about the chief's bad habit. At least he wasn't clipping them this morning and lining up the pieces, mused O'Malley. "And I spoke to Public Works," O'Malley continued to explain to the chief. "They're working on clearing storm drains to alleviate the flooding around town. By the way, my buddy from Staten Island called. His house is gone; his entire neighborhood is gone. Boy did the Cape ever dodge that bullet or what!"

"Tell me when Partridge gets back here and keep me up to date on all the reports," muttered the chief. "And what's the status on power outages. That damn power company better get its act together on this storm. We dodged the bullet, so I won't stand for outages lasting two weeks like after the last storm. Get them on the phone," and he grumbled as he gnawed at his fingernail once more.

Partridge glanced at Cotter as he got out of the cruiser and said, "Here we are at Northridge again. And can you believe it's another murder investigation? How long ago was that case where the housekeeper's boyfriend killed one of the residents here? You know, the guy with a whole criminal life hidden until the murder."

"You mean the Jerry Smith case? I sure remember that," said Cotter. "You hadn't been on the force for that long, and you had this big city attitude that drove me and everyone else crazy. You still drive me crazy when you act like you know everything, but you're getting better. A little more training from me and the rest of the force, plus a few kicks in the head when needed, and maybe we'll accept you as one of our own," and he grinned at Partridge while giving him a friendly slap on the back.

"Still a little sensitive I see," laughed Partridge. "I'll try to behave. Don't want you and the others intimidated by my big city attitude. Now let's get in there and see what's going on."

Rinaldo had been the first officer on site. He reported that he had taken preliminary statements from Mrs. Weinberger, the neighbor and friend who had discovered the victim. He stated that he had also taken statements from her husband who had been dragged into the crime scene to verify what she had seen. Rinaldo had cordoned off the area and his cruiser was parked in the driveway to further secure the location. When Partridge and Cotter pulled up the next morning, it was still raining hard but the winds had died down.

"Rinaldo," said Partridge, "how's it going? Quite a storm. Took us a while to get here. Sorry about that. Cotter here nearly got himself killed. Must have heard about it over the radio. A tree landed on his patrol car. Nearly destroyed it."

"Hell of a rough night," said Cotter. "I'm on my way to the station when this monster of a tree crashes down on me. Had to wait for Partridge here to come and get me. Real slow going out there this morning, too. I guess it'll be one for the books. Don't remember the last time a hurricane hit us, but we're lucky compared to reports been hearing out of New York and Jersey. Got a brother over on the shore. Sister-in-law told the wife their house is gone. What a mess. Well anyway, what do we have here?"

Rinaldo filled Partridge and Cotter in on all the details. "Mrs. Weinberger's a mess. She's the one discovered the body. She and the husband heard a crash and went out to examine the damage from the tree that landed on top of their car over there. Mrs. Weinberger goes to check on the victim, figuring the crash must have scared her. Seems they have this mother-daughter relationship going on. That's when she discovers the body, runs out to get her husband, who verifies what she saw, and they call us. The medical examiner left here about an hour ago. Had quite a hair raising story himself about getting here, but I'll let him tell you all about it. You know how he likes to tell a good story, so I won't ruin it for him. He took extensive photographs, so I guess it's up to you guys to wrap thing up now. I've already completed what I need for the preliminary report."

Partridge and Cotter thanked Rinaldo. They put on paper booties to preserve evidence and entered the house.

"Cotter, check the slider for anything suspicious," said Partridge. "My guess is the perp came in through the front door. We know, according to what Mrs. Weinberger told Rinaldo, that the victim always left her front door open. Maybe she even knew the assailant."

"Nothing suspicious," yelled Cotter. "No sign of entry, and the area around the door is still dry. With this weather, even if the guy took off his shoes, there'd be dripping off his clothes from that awful rain we had."

"So we know he probably entered and left through the front door," said Partridge. "Radio is still on in the bathroom. Probably why she didn't hear him enter. Guy trashed the house, probably after killing her. I'd say it wasn't a robbery, what with that nice painting still on the wall, the lap top over there on the floor, and that nice watch next to it. We'll have to get Mrs. Weinberger in here to check out the place and see if anything is missing. Guess she knew the woman real well and was here a lot. She should be able to give us a list of Rafferty's friends and acquaintances and the woman's daily activities. Any dramatic change might be a clue here."

"That storm was a good cover for this crime." said Cotter. "No tire tracks or anything outside to follow up on. This is going to be a tough one."

"You think so? Think outside the box for Christ's sake," said Partridge. "Maybe the guy didn't arrive by limo. Maybe he arrived on foot. Maybe he even lives here. Maybe he used the front door because he knew it was always open. Now that should give us a hell of a lot to go on!"

"Thanks for the big city analysis," said Cotter. "Think you're stretching my words a little? For Christ's sake, yourself. I'm the one who should be acting bitchy right now, not you. I'm the one who nearly got killed and lost a cruiser. What's your excuse?"

"Got it," said Partridge, "but sometimes you act so dumb it sets me off. There's a hell of a lot to go on here. We've got the direction of the knife wounds letting us know if the guy is right or left handed. Got some partial footprints on the carpet. Probably have some fingerprints where the room was trashed, and we've an idea that maybe the guy walked here. That's a lot of angles to check on. Want me to elaborate further, or do you think we've enough to keep us busy?

"What time is it anyway?" he went on. "I want to get next door and interview the Weinbergers. Crazy how they're involved in this murder too. They must live under a black cloud or something. Especially the Mrs. But seems this time a sweet old lady is killed rather than a creep like that Jerry Smith."

Partridge and Cotter walked over to the Weinberger's home and knocked on the door. It was 9 a.m.

"Probably won't be waking them up," said Cotter. "Old people don't sleep late. And what with the murder of a neighbor and that storm, they probably didn't sleep much at all."

"Might be right," said Partridge. "Funny, when you're a kid you want to sleep, but your parents always wake you up. Then, when you get older, you can't sleep. Crazy how that happens. I think it should be the other way around. You know, when you're older, sleep should come easily. Oh well, that's life. Sure is taking a long time for someone to answer that door. Maybe we are waking them up."

Partridge knocked again. The power was still out, so the doorbell wasn't working. He glanced at the tree that was now covering the Weinberger's car. "What a shame," he said pointing in the direction of the car. "We were damn lucky here on the Cape from everything I've been hearing."

Judy answered the door after the second knock. "Hello. I can't believe this. Please come in." And then she started to cry. "Mary was such a wonderful neighbor and friend. How could this have happened?" She wiped her eyes and blew her nose. "Were you at the door very long? I was in the bathroom, and Phil was sleeping. There's nothing to do without power, so he decided to sleep a little bit later. We're usually early risers. Phil will be out in a minute; he's putting on some clothes. Sorry I can't offer you coffee or anything. Do you happen to know when we might get our power back?"

"Sorry Mrs. Weinberger, but we don't," answered Cotter. "But as someone who has lived with power outages in this town too many times, I hope the power company has their act together for this storm. They certainly were well aware before it struck."

Judy had been reading for hours and still was not finished when Partridge and Cotter knocked at the door. Detectives at her door about the murder of yet another friend seemed like a bad dream. Whoever heard of people like them involved in a murder investigation, let alone two she thought. Judy knew she had to listen to Phil and finish the diaries. She knew he was right when he said she would be withholding information from a murder investigation if she did not turn them over. She wondered if Phil would miss her if she went to jail, and cringed at her crazy thoughts. Jail was certainly not going to happen, she told herself, so any thoughts of whether Phil would miss her were ridiculous. But she did have to somehow speed up the reading and get the diaries to the detectives.

"Oh good, here's Phil," said Judy while trying to quiet her own thoughts. "Phil, can you believe it's Detectives Partridge and Cotter in our house investigating another crime? Oh God, and this time it's someone I loved," and she began to cry once again.

Phil put his arm around her and tried to offer comfort. She cried quietly and attempted to wipe her tears and blow her nose with a crumpled tissue that had probably been used too many times already. "Honey, try to relax. The detectives are here now, and we need to tell them everything we know about Mary. Do you want me to get you a glass of water?"

"Sure, but don't open the fridge. I want to preserve the cold in there as long as possible. Who knows how long it will take to get the power back."

"Thanks for the warning, but I think I'm smart enough to know that I need to get water from the sink."

Judy gave him a sideward glance of annoyance and said, "I know that. But given your age and how forgetful you are, I thought you might have gone right to the fridge without thinking. Sorry detectives, just a little chatter between the two of us. We've been married a long time, and we often wrangle back and forth. It doesn't mean anything."

"Not to worry," smiled Cotter. "Me and the Mrs. are at it ourselves sometimes. May we sit down? We have some questions. We hope you have information that will help us find out what happened to Mrs. Rafferty."

Judy tried not to glance at Phil, but she could feel his eyes bearing down on her. She was not going to give up the diaries or say anything about them. They had been entrusted to her, and she was not through reading them. She took a deep breath, reached into her pocket for another crumpled tissue, and tried to smile at the detectives. "Please sit down. Let me move these blankets and this battery operated lantern. I've been out here reading all night. Couldn't sleep what with the wind and that awful rain banging against the windows. Phil can sleep anywhere. Nothing bothers him."

"What are you reading? asked Partridge. My girlfriend loves to read. She's always looking for a recommendation."

"I don't remember the title. It's in the other room. It's pretty good. A friend told me to read it. Have to return it to the library real soon, so I was up reading all night. Kept me busy. Phil told me to come to bed, but I kept reading." She knew she was mumbling, and she tried to calm down as she crossed the room and sat next to her husband.

"Don't worry about the title," smiled Partridge. "We just have a few questions for both of you."

When Partridge smiled, she saw a few black seeds stuck between his front teeth. She wondered if he had just eaten a poppy seed bagel and if he got it at Panera's or at the bagel shop. The thought of seeds stuck between his teeth relaxed her. She needed to stay calm if she was to answer questions and not reveal the fact that she was hiding diaries that could contain important information. She took another deep breath and looked at the detectives. "What can we do to help? We can't believe this. Mary and I were very close. She was like a mother to me. I liked her from the moment she moved next door. You know how sometimes you instantly connect with a person. You can't explain it.

It's like you've known that person your entire life. They're easy to talk to, and they understand you."

"Judy, let the detectives talk. They want to ask us questions, and you're rambling on and on."

Partridge jumped in. "Not a problem, Mr. Weinberger. It's all important information for us. Now let's start at the beginning. Mrs. Weinberger, take your time. How did you discover Mrs. Rafferty?"

Somehow she got through the interview. Phil was great. He sat next to her and squeezed her hand several times to keep her grounded. He even did most of the talking, which also helped to calm her.

She became surprised, following the questioning, when Detective Partridge told her he had a lead on some of the missing items from the Northridge clubhouse. She had forgotten she and another resident were working with the police to discover who had taken them.

Partridge said, "A man was arrested a few days ago in connection with a break-in at a home on the lower Cape. The police there executed a search warrant at the suspect's house and found thousands of dollars worth of items believed to have been stolen from area homes and businesses. Two of the paintings found matched those stolen from the clubhouse here, and the police feel there's a strong possibility another person was also involved. We'll get back to you and Max about that situation when we have more information."

When the detectives left, Phil said, "If you don't finish the diaries today, I'm going to take them and call the police myself. I had enough of your involvement when Jerry was killed. I'm not going through that aggravation again. You can't keep them hidden forever. They could hold the key to who killed Mary."

Judy knew he was right, as much as she hated to admit so. "I'll finish them today," she said. "We'll call the detectives tomorrow and tell them we forgot all about the diaries in the confusion of the murder and the storm."

"You better finish them today. I mean it Judy."

"Don't tell me what I better do!" Judy screamed. "I already said I'd finish today and then we'd call them. I heard you the first time. Just leave me alone," and she ran into the bedroom and slammed the door behind her. Sometimes he drove her crazy. She wondered why she always let him bait her.

"Don't you slam the door on me!" he screamed back. "Finish today, or I take them."

She didn't answer. The lack of a response would infuriate him, and that was her goal. He had made her angry, and now she wanted to do the same to him. It drove him crazy when he baited her, and she didn't answer back. It had taken her a long time to figure that out, and she loved when she could use that knowledge. Let him stew a little, she thought to herself, and she grabbed a diary and began to read again . . .

Dear Diary,

I contacted Jennie when I got to New York. I wanted to know what Joey did when he found out I ran away along with all his money, my money . . .

"He went crazy when he discovered you were gone. He tried to get to me," Jennie said, "but of course I didn't open my door. He was screaming and swearing and even tried kicking in the door. A couple guys held him down til the police came. It was pretty ugly. I understand they threw him in jail after giving him a pretty good beating. The police here protect us and don't take his kind of violence lightly. They even got him for trying to entice girls younger than eighteen to work for him. I'm pretty sure they'll put him away for quite a while. Be careful! He said if he found you, he was going to kill you. You know him better than I do, but I'd watch my back if I were you."

Mary thanked Jennie for being such a good friend. "Don't worry about me Jennie. I'm safe now."

She had never been to New York, and she was like a little kid staring up at the tall buildings. Her saviors had brought her there and away from Joey, but they were not there to take care of her. They did, however, give her a place to stay for a few days until she could get on her feet. She did not know how she was going to manage. She had all the money she had taken from Joey, and it was a great deal, but she did not want to spend it. She remembered some of the men in Miami talking about how they invested their money, and she thought doing that made sense. She hoped the Nesbitts would help her find the right people. But for now, she put it all in the bank and only took a small amount out for living expenses. Mary needed help, and *A New Way* was the name of a Christian supported organization that supported women like her. She heard about them from the Nesbitts who brought her to her first meeting. The group helped her get job training and accept who she was and who she could become. It was a chance to change her life. They even taught her secretarial skills and helped her get a job in an office. If it was not for that program, she knew she would have gone right back to life as a prostitute. It was the only one she had known.

Dear Diary,

I stayed in New York for several years, but it was hard trying to live a new kind of life. I was thirty years old, living in Queens, New York, and holding down a very low paying office job. The people in the office were kind to me, and I stayed in touch with the Nesbitts, but I was miserable. Sure I was safe, but I wanted nice things. I had been without them in Amsterdam because Joey kept all my money, but when I was in Miami . . . oh what beautiful presents I used to get. And the food, what food. I used to be taken to the finest restaurants as payment for my company. The presents and the restaurants used to make Joey really mad. Where's the damn money he would scream. Tell them you want money not presents. Now that I was managing my own money, I wanted to have those nice things again. So I started selling off some of the stocks the Nesbitts helped me buy . . .

Mary was not disciplined, and the money from Amsterdam began to disappear. She panicked. Alone except for the Nesbitts, a few friends, *A New Way,* and her low paying job—she wondered how she would survive in New York. Her life there, a boring life of routine, made her think of the life she left in Florida when she ran away from home. She didn't want to go back to that life, but Florida had also been good to her. It had brought her an introduction to the finer things. She thought that now, without Joey, maybe she could go back to that life. She was still young. Maybe she could start up again as an escort. The people at *A New Way* wouldn't approve, but they didn't understand her. And so she said goodbye to the Nesbitts, quit her job, and cut her ties with *A New Way.*

CHAPTER 4

The ride back to the station to file their report took Partridge and Cotter twenty minutes instead of the usual five. Route 151 was almost at a dead stop. There were fallen trees in the road, and the curious were out in their cars. The new guy, fresh out of training, was directing traffic and trying to move the gawkers along. When he spotted the detectives, he stopped traffic to let them by and saluted as they passed.

"Seems like a good kid," said Cotter. "Spent a few minutes with him the other day. He's from out around Framingham somewhere. Said he's got an aunt who lives on the Cape. Always visited here as a kid, so he thought it might be a good place to raise a family. Hey, how's life going with Cynthia? You don't seem to talk about her lately."

"Going great. Not much to say. Enjoy each other's company, her kids are great, they seem to like me . . . that's about it."

"Think you might marry again someday?" asked Cotter. "I mean you two evidently like each other, and you get along with her kids. You thinking of asking her?"

"What's this twenty questions all of a sudden? I don't plan on rushing into anything. What we've got works for the two of us. Situation changes, I'll be sure to let you know. For now it's status quo and a very happy status quo, by the way. Now stop yapping and start thinking about that murder. We've a few good places to start. First, I'd like to talk to the guard at the gate and find out who drove into Northridge during the storm. Then, I'd like to compare that information to the time of death from the medical examiner. Since there was no forced entry, we already agreed she might have known her assailant. Or maybe, somehow, the assailant knew she always kept her door open. Of course there's always the possibility whoever it was randomly chose a house to burgle, and their plan went wrong. My bet is on someone she knew."

Cotter nodded in agreement. "I tend to agree. But who? The neighbor, Mrs. Weinberger, seems to be the closest friend, and she and her husband say the victim didn't have any known friends or relatives. Seems pretty strange to me, like she was hiding something."

"I'd like to go back and question the Weinbergers," said Partridge. "Remember, we worked with them on the Jerry Smith case and the Mrs. withheld some information. Just a hunch based on past experience, but I'd like to question her a bit more. Maybe I can prod more out of her or at least scratch her memory a bit. Maybe the victim said something that Mrs. Weinberger forgot. First let's see the chief, fill him in, and then get a bite to eat. I'm starving. What about you?"

"Now that you mention it, I haven't eaten for hours. Spent all that time with my crushed cruiser and forgot to even grab a coffee. Sounds like a plan to me. Lead the way boss."

"Oh now I'm the boss. When did that promotion take place?" Partridge smiled at Cotter and saluted. "I'll remember that when I need to push you around a little," and he chuckled to himself.

"Think I'll demote you," Cotter said, "if this is going

to make you more obnoxious then you already are," and he saluted back. "Hey, all kidding aside, where should we go for coffee? Actually, I think I want a big breakfast. Maybe we can make our way over to Moonikis if Route 28 up there isn't too bad. Love the pancakes even though they're kind of expensive."

"Dream on Cotter. Look at the weather. Look at the traffic. Think about the chief's reaction. Do you really think Moonakis is a good idea right now? Tell you what. We solve this case in a reasonable time, or whenever it's solved, I treat you to a big breakfast at Moonakis. You know, to celebrate our new relationship of boss and underling. We can call it a bribe so you won't demote me. For now, what do you say we grab a bagel after we talk with the chief? Maybe that will help your growling stomach, which is really starting to annoy me."

"Sorry boss," and he sheepishly looked at Partridge as they both started to laugh.

The station was busy, almost a mad house. Phones were ringing everywhere, and the chief's shouting was evident the minute they walked in. "Where in damnation were you guys? There's been a storm around here case you haven't noticed. Everyone's helping out, but don't see or hear from you two all morning. Where've you been? Find out you went to breakfast, and you'll both be back on the street directing traffic. Now get the hell in my office."

Partridge glanced at Cotter and said, "What's up with him this morning? Doesn't he know we're on the murder case over at Northridge?" and he followed Cotter into the chief's office.

"Shut the damn door, Cotter. With all the noise out there, how can anyone think? Now where the hell you guys been?" They watched as he settled into his chair, grabbed his nail clippers, and proceeded to study his nails. "What are you staring at? I asked a question, now give me an answer, damn it. Partridge, I'm waiting."

"Over at Northridge, Chief. You remember, there was a murder over there, and you assigned the case to us."

"Don't get fresh with me," the chief snarled. Fill me in, and I haven't got all day.

Partridge bit his tongue and answered. "We've examined the grounds and the inside of the house for evidence, and we've also spoken with the State Police Emergency Response Team, as well as the medical examiner. We found the victim in her bathtub. Had one of those emergency radios playing, so probably didn't hear the perp til it was too late. The house was trashed. Appears to have entered through the front door. No sign of a break-in, and the slider, the only other entrance to the house, was still locked. We've interviewed the neighbors, the Weinbergers. They told us the victim always kept her door unlocked. Might have known her killer. Might have even been a resident of Northridge. Lot to check into here. Planning to have Mrs. Weinberger check the house to see if anything is missing . . . you know, money, jewelry, the likes. They were very close."

"Why's that name sound so familiar?" the chief said while continuing to clip his nails.

"They were friends of that Jerry Smith guy who was found dead near the pond in Northridge. Remember we discovered that Smith had killed his wife while they were on vacation in the islands," said Cotter.

"Right, remember that now. So how are the Weinbergers involved this time? What are they the lead team for murder over at Northridge?" and the chief laughed.

"Well," said Partridge while smiling at the chief's joke, "the Mrs. was a good friend of the victim. They were neighbors, and we understand they had this close mother-daughter relationship. The Weinbergers told us the victim had no family and never wanted to search the Internet for any relatives. Mr. Weinberger always thought that was strange, but Mrs. Weinberger hadn't been concerned. Also, Mrs. Weinberger held back some information during the Jerry Smith investigation, so maybe she's doing the same here. Who knows. I'm going to push her a little and see if I get anywhere."

"I remember those people from Northridge," said the chief. "They nearly drove me crazy with their constant calls and questions during the Jerry Smith investigation. I don't need that this time. Solve the damn thing ASAP, and for Christ's sake keep me in the loop. I don't want to go searching for you. If you get something, anything, get back to me right away. Hey Cotter, any news about your cruiser? Maybe I'll charge the replacement to you for not keeping your eyes on the road. Now scram, both of you."

CHAPTER 5

Judy was preoccupied by thoughts of Mary's funeral. She knew that she and Phil would be involved in the arrangements and that she would speak at the service. Her head was spinning. "First things first," she told herself. "You need to finish the diaries in the next twenty-four hours and hand them over to the detectives. Phil was serious when he said he would take them from you tomorrow, and you still have several left to read." She decided to skim the remaining diaries in an attempt to move through them more quickly. With the bedroom door closed and Phil probably fuming on the other side, she resumed her reading . . .

Dear Diary

I moved back to Miami and my old life as an escort. I was happy. Good restaurants, gifts, and plenty of cash were once again a part of my world. Before long I met Frank. He was handsome, wealthy, and generous in every way. I spent all my free time with him and even thought I was in love. I wondered if he was the man who could become my husband and the father of my children. How very foolish I was. No, how very stupid I was. He had other plans in mind and became physically abusive when I refused to go into prostitution for him. Frank had forced several women to work for him, and I was just the next one on his list. I was devastated, angry, and determined to get even. My chance came when I was approached by the police, who had been watching him for some time. They wanted to trap him in a sting operation, and I was more than willing to help put him away for years. After Frank, there were a few quiet years when I worked exclusively for clients I knew. I also started to save and invest my money.

During those quiet years, I had time to reflect on my life with both Joey and Frank. I realized how dangerous it would be if either of them came back to Miami and found me. When one of my clients told me about Las Vegas and assured me that I would love life there, I listened and moved. I also changed my name to Sheila Nichols to further protect myself. The paper-work supporting my name change was easy with all the people I knew who worked both sides of what was legal. With my new name and a new home, I was feeling less vulnerable.

I took a job at The Sands Hotel and was paid to hang around the crap tables, push drinks, and encourage the big rollers to bet. The pay was great, and there was always an opportunity for generous tips from the big spenders. The bouncer at the hotel liked me, and he was often there late at night to drive me home. It certainly beat taking a cab.

Smitty had been a boxer, but not a great one, so he didn't last very long on the circuit. He arrived in Vegas to make a big score but ended up getting the shit kicked out of him. With his looks both gruff and imposing, he had easily moved out of the ring and into the bouncer business. I met him when he arrived at The Sands to replace a guy who got his face pushed in when he was caught trying to steal from the casino. Smitty was kind, friendly, and asked absolutely nothing of me which was a big change from all the other men in my life. Smitty and I soon became a number out on the strip—we were like an old married couple. After a short time we moved in with one another and set up our household. It was a good life. We both worked nights, so we slept in mornings. I guess you could say we played house. Neither of us had ever been married, and we never talked about doing so. We were a married couple in every way but legally, and we were happy in our present arrangement without the commitment and ugliness often associated with marriage. They were good years and as close to real happiness as I ever experienced. And then it all ended . . .

"What do you mean you have to leave?" I said to him on that hot and dry Monday morning. "Where are you going?" I was confused. We had been together for five years, and we had never had this kind of conversation.

"They're after me babe. They think I ratted on one of the big guys, and I'm on everyone's hit list."

"Well tell them," I said while beginning to panic. "Tell them you aren't a rat. Tell them you don't know anything, and you aren't a rat."

"Sheila, Sheila baby. You've been in this town for a lot of years and on the gutter side of life for even more years, but honey you are so naive. Do you think they're going to say . . . 'Okay Smitty. Guess we were wrong You're cool?' Of course not! They think I ratted, and what they think is all that matters. I'm leaving in a few minutes. Staying around any longer will put you in danger. That way, when they come searching for me, you can tell them I was gone when you woke up."

"How will I manage without you Smitty? You've been the best thing that ever happened to me."

"Don't cry, just listen to me," Smitty said. "I have a safe-deposit box at the bank that I've never told you about. Here's the key. Your name is on all the paper work. If everything works out, I mean if everything is quiet after six months or so, go to the box. You'll find a letter telling you how to reach me with enough money in there to take care of you if you can't reach me. These guys don't fool around, and they don't care if I did or didn't do what they said I did. The only truth they believe is their truth. Tell them I ripped you off, we had a big fight, and I left. Tell them you want a piece of the bastard if they find me. Take care honey. I hope our paths cross again soon. You've also been the best thing that ever happened to me."

And then he was gone without giving her a chance to respond or ask questions. He simply walked out the door. She never saw him again. He was found a few days later tied to one of the steel beams of a building under construction. His body had been burned. Was he innocent? Was he what they said he was? She didn't know, but she had loved him, and she had believed him, and now she was scared to death. She took the money out of the safe-deposit box along with his letter and left Vegas. If they could do this to him, one of the sweetest guys in the world, they could do anything, even to her. Because they knew her as Sheila, she decided to become Mary once again. She hoped that she would be lucky and that they would never search for her. But she was scared. She was scared of the guys who killed Smitty, scared of Frank finding her when he got out of jail, and scared of Joey if he ever located her. She was now in her early forties with big tastes for the good life, no skills, and the fear that her past could catch up with her.

Dear Diary,

I didn't know where to go or what to do. It amazed me that at my age I was still screwing up. Other women had careers, families, people who cared about them. Me, I had nothing. Sure, I had some money. I had invested wisely with the help of a stock-broker, and I had Smitty's money from the safe-deposit box, but what else did I have? I packed what was important, left everything else including Sheila behind, and drove to California. I hoped the fresh air and new surroundings would shake me out of my depression and help me find a new direction . . .

CHAPTER 6

"Well, did you finish the damn diaries?" Phil shouted as he came out of the bathroom. "I said you had until today to hand them over to the detectives. If you don't, I will."

"I said I'd tell them, and I will. I need a little more time. Today isn't over. There's a lot to digest. I'll call them later today or tomorrow. I promise. Don't bug me. I'm not a child. I said I would, and I will. The reading will be easier now that the power is back. But I need to stretch, I need a change of scenery, and I need a cup of coffee. There isn't any in the house. Let's get some breakfast, and then I'll come back and finish. I promise. I'm heartbroken over Mary's death and anxious for the police to find her killer. And I'm a little overwhelmed about arrangements for her funeral and my need to speak since I knew her best. That's a lot on my plate, don't you think. So give me some slack."

"Sorry. I guess that's a lot to digest. Coffee and a bagel might help clear your head a little. But don't forget about the tree on top of the car. We'll have to walk."

"The walk will be good. It'll help me relax so I can think more clearly. That means you're giving me a little slack, right?"

"Right," Phil grumbled with not much conviction.

"Say it like you mean it Phil. I need your support here, not your sarcasm. So say right."

"Yeah, yeah . . . right. Now get dressed, and let's get out of here for a couple hours."

They'd barely moved out of the driveway when they started to see neighbors. Everyone was talking about the hurricane as well as Mary's murder.

"Judy, oh my God Judy! That was your neighbor who was killed, wasn't it? How awful. I heard you were really friendly with her. You must be in shock."

"Hi Phyllis," said Judy. "I think you know my husband, Phil. Phil, you remember Phyllis. She lives next door to the Grays on Wheeler Circle."

"Sure, sure. Your husband is Pete, right? I was on a committee with him once. Hard worker. Tell him I said hello."

"Judy, if you want that bagel, we better get moving. You know how early they run out, and it's a long walk."

"Are you two walking all the way over there? How come you aren't driving? It's going to be a long walk trying to dodge all the downed trees and other junk that's been pushed to the side of the road?"

"Well," said Phil, "we've got a tree down on our car, so we can't get our other car out of the garage."

"You could borrow our car. I'm sure Pete wouldn't mind. I can call him right now on my new smartphone. Do you guys have one of these? I don't know how I got along without one. We stayed connected all through the storm. Pete kept plugging it into that car thingy-doo when the battery looked like it was dying. I tweeted and emailed all over the place. It was amazing how much information I was able to get, and it sure helped pass the time."

"Thanks Phyllis, but Judy and I need the walk. It's been a hard time at our house, and we need to decompress."

"Holler if you change your mind," she said.

The walk turned out to be a nightmare. They kept running into neighbors who had heard of Mary's death and wanted all the details. After a few minutes, Judy had had enough.

"That's it. I can't stand another minute of this. Get me out of here Phil. I want to clear my head, but I don't want to keep discussing Mary's murder with everyone who passes me on the street."

"We should've realized this would happen. Do you want me to call someone to come and get us? I could call Chuck or Don. Either one would pick us up in a minute. Wait. Isn't that Max's house over there? What if I run in and ask him. I don't know him that well, but the two of you've been working with the police on those disappearances from the clubhouse. I'm sure he'd help you."

"I feel funny asking, but I'm really desperate. Alright, let's both knock on the door."

They borrowed a car from Max after a short conversation and made their way to the bagel shop. Luckily no one there knew them, and Judy started to relax a bit after her first few sips of coffee. Phil was smart, and he didn't discuss the diary or the murder. They simply sat there and talked about the storm and mundane everyday topics. It was a little forced, but they both seemed to unwind a little.

"Judy, I think we should head back now. We told Max we wouldn't keep his car that long, and we've been here over an hour. And besides, you know you have to finish reading those diaries."

"I know. I know. But it feels so good to get out of the house and away from the nightmare. Thank you for not discussing it. I'm almost finished with the diaries and then I promise I'll call Detective Partridge."

Phil smiled at Judy and said, "Sorry I've been so hard on you, but this is serious business, and I don't want us involved anymore than we already are. I'll drop you off so you don't have to walk back from Max's house."

"That's a good idea. Thanks for thinking of it. I love you. And I'm sorry I was on your case, but you know how close I was to Mary, and . . ."

"I know. I know. We've both been on edge."

Phil dropped Judy at the bottom of the driveway and left to return Max's car. There were several workmen close to the garage engaged in removing the large tree that had fallen across their car. She and Phil had seen them all over Northridge removing the branches and large tree limbs that had fallen during the storm. Some of the men were with the Northridge landscape and maintenance crew, but others were day workers brought in for the cleanup. The sound of buzz saws was deafening. As she opened her front door, Judy glanced at Mary's house, which was still cordoned off with yellow police tape

She screamed when she walked into the living room. Furniture was knocked over, sofa cushions were on the floor, drawers were upturned, and all Mary's diaries were missing. Someone had been there, and she quickly realized they could still be in the house. Judy was trembling as she ran out of the house and used her cell to call 911. Detectives Partridge and Cotter were nearby and arrived within minutes. Phil arrived right behind them.

"Mrs. Weinberger," said Partridge, "you'd better start from the beginning because this is obviously related to your neighbor's murder."

"I knew it. I told her," said Phil. "I told her to turn the diaries over as soon as we discovered Mary's body. I told her she was interfering with the police investigation. But no, she needed to read them first. She needed to play detective."

"Please calm down Mr. Weinberger," said Detective Partridge. "We'll take over from here. Mrs. Weinberger, withholding evidence is serious. We could file charges."

Judy started to cry, and Phil glared at her while

shaking his head.

"But I'm not going to do that," said Partridge. "I'm going to forget that you withheld information. Now let's start from the beginning, and please make sure you tell us everything. I'm sure I don't have to tell you how serious this is."

After composing herself, Judy explained how Mary had given her a letter. "She told me to put it in a safe place and not to read it unless something happened to her, like if she died. She also gave me a box," said Judy "She told me if anything happened to her, she wanted me to read the letter first. She said it would explain what was in the box. She said it would all belong to me, and I was to decide what to do with the contents. So I read the letter and then opened the box. It was filled with her diaries. I was in the process of reading them, and I was almost finished when Phil and I left the house. You see, I had run out of coffee before the storm and never had a chance to go shopping. Phil thought a cup of coffee would help me clear my head. And then someone broke in while we were out, and all the diaries were stolen. I'm sorry. I really am. I loved that woman, and I only wanted to know more about her.

Detectives, she had a terrible life. She said . . . she said . . . oh God, it's so awful. I still can't believe what I read. She said she was a prostitute, and she said she was a thief too. But I loved her, so I kept reading because I thought I might find out who killed her. I guess I was wrong keeping the information from you," and she glanced at Phil.

"You sure were," Phil snickered. "You never listen. You always think you know everything, and now someone's broken into our home. Jesus Christ, Judy."

"What's done is done," said Partridge. "Obviously you should have shared the information, Mrs. Weinberger. We already said we wouldn't press charges, but please understand what you did could be considered obstruction of justice, which carries a sentence of up to five years in prison."

"See," gasped Phil with obvious exasperation. "Judy, will you ever learn? What happens now, detectives? I know she didn't think she was interfering with your investigation, and she had promised me she would turn the letter and diaries over to you as soon as she finished reading them."

Judy looked at Phil and smiled at him through her tears. "I want this nightmare to end. I know I should have listened to my husband when he told me to give you the diaries. But I simply wanted to learn more about someone I loved. You understand, don't you?"

"Although we understand your reasoning, Mrs. Weinberger, we hope you now realize it was wrong not to immediately tell us about the diaries and the accompanying letter. Now we have another crime—your robbery. As we told you previously, this may have been committed by someone in Northridge or someone connected in some way with Northridge. We need you to come down to the station within the next hour and tell us everything you can recall about Mary Rafferty's life from reading her diaries. You too, Mr. Weinberger, because the Mrs. discussed some of what she read with you."

With that, the two detectives left the Weinberger home and drove out of Northridge. "We better get back to the chief and fill him in," said Partridge.

"Think he's going to yell and scream about the robbery? You know . . . blame us for not questioning the Weinbergers in more detail and for not realizing they were hiding something?"

"Who do you think I am, a fortune teller? How the hell do I know what the chief is going to do. He certainly won't be happy, that's for sure, but even you should be able to figure that one out."

"Quit the sarcasm," said Cotter. "You know there are

other detectives I could partner with . . . others who would appreciate me."

"Appreciate you?" grinned Partridge. "The next thing you'll be asking me to do is love you, as well as appreciate you. Sorry, no deal." They arrived at the station a short time later and immediately ran into the chief, who had been looking for them.

"Into my office, you two. Seems like I'm always looking for you. Why is that? Don't tell me. You'll just waste more of my time. So how come you guys always have cases over at Northridge with this Weinberger dame?"

Partridge quickly briefed the chief on the burglary and Mrs. Weinberger's withholding of evidence.

"Let me see if I've got this right so far," said the chief. "First we find her friend Jerry Smith dead, then she's involved in the investigation of mysterious disappearances from their clubhouse, then her neighbor—some old lady who Weinberger says is like a mother to her—is found murdered, next you report that she kept important evidence from us, and now I'm told it was stolen when her house was burgled. What the fuck is it with that woman! Shit, wouldn't want to be her friend," and he laughed at his own joke, bringing on his cigarette cough.

CHAPTER 7

"Why are you here?" she said. "What if someone recognizes the car."

"I'm not stupid," he said. "The car's at the Commons. I walked over."

"Did you find anything at the Weinberger's? Shit, what a mess. Why did I ever agree to help you? I want out of here. I'm not going to prison for helping you kill her. You said it would be easy. You said you'd only scare her. You said she'd hand the stuff over. I'm frightened!"

"Shut-up! Just shut-up and stay cool. They don't know anything about us, and there's no way they'll find out. Keep on doing what you're doing. Talk about your kids or grandkids. Say you wish you lived closer to them. Then, if you have to leave in a hurry, people will think you went to visit them."

"But I don't have kids or grandkids stupid. Remember . . . I told everyone that I've never been married!"

"Don't ever call me stupid again! You hear me?" and he slapped her. "Just do what I say. Start telling a story, any story about why you haven't mentioned grandkids before. And yes, I did find what I was looking for. Found a bunch of diaries with her handwriting. I'd recognize them anywhere. Used to tease her about all that damn writing. Said it helped her remember stuff. Joked with her about it one time. Said if she ever wrote about me, I'd have to kill her. Think she believed it. That dame knew too much about all of us. Probably why she disappeared. Never thought I'd find her after all these years. Now the reward will be even bigger after I blackmail him. Once I find what I need in those diaries, I'll be on easy street."

Touching her cheek, she eyed him but didn't say a word. She wondered if he would kill her like he had killed Mary Rafferty. "Alright, I'll do what you say. Just don't run off and leave me holding the bag."

"Don't tell me what to do," he screamed, and walked out the door. "Damn women," he said to himself. "They're always telling you what to do. Can't live with them and can't live without them. But, if you're smart, you get rid of them when necessary and learn how to live without them," and he grinned as he walked away.

CHAPTER 8

"Chief," said Cotter, "can I get you water for that cough?"

"May I, Cotter. May I. My sister was an English teacher, and she drilled that one into me. Can means are you capable of performing the task. May means do I have your permission. I assume you meant to say may," and he laughed, which aggravated his cough even more.

"Don't say assume," said Cotter. "You know what they say about people who assume . . . if you assume, you make an ass out of you and me! Get it?"

"Thanks for the clarification Cotter," snickered the chief. "I wasn't born yesterday? Just do your damn job."

"Sorry. Didn't mean to annoy you."

"Right," said the chief. "Okay, so what's the next step already?"

Partridge winked at Cotter and said, "We're planning to question the Weinbergers about the diaries. Actually they're due here within the hour. Mrs. Weinberger's really the one who read them. She only shared a few parts with her husband. Hope to get more information about the deceased from what they remember. Soon as we finish the interview, we'll fill you in unless you want to be there."

"You two handle it. That's why you're detectives."

CHAPTER 9

Judy wasn't going to change, but she decided to put on a clean pair of jeans and a different sweater.

"Why are you changing?" said Phil. "You looked fine. This isn't a social engagement. They aren't looking at you; they're only listening to you."

"Thanks for the usual sarcasm. You never disappoint. I'm changing because I feel sweaty, and I look grubby. I was still wearing what I had on yesterday when I found Mary. But you wouldn't notice. You never notice what I have on or how I look."

"Instead of lecturing me," said Phil, "you'd do better to concentrate on yourself and get dressed. You're in enough trouble already without making the detectives wait for you."

A second later the phone rang, and Judy answered. "Hello, oh hi Shirley. I can't talk. Phil and I are on our way out."

Phil motioned to Judy and whispered, "Tell her you'll call her later. Why did you answer? God Judy, we've got to go!"

"Shirley, we've got to go. I'll call you back."

"Wait, don't hang up. I just heard about Mary. With the storm and no phone service as well as a dead cell phone, we've been out of touch here. Maureen came by and told me about Mary's murder and the robbery at your house. She couldn't believe that we didn't know. Is it true? Are you alright?"

"It's true Shirley. It's been awful. We've been questioned by the police, and we're on our way over to the station now. I can't talk. Phil is screaming at me to hang up. I'm a wreck. I'll call you and Maureen when I can."

Shirley hung up and told Chuck that what Maureen had told them was all correct.

"Wonder why she didn't call you or Maureen," said Chuck. "I thought you were all such good friends. You're all still speaking aren't you? No one had a fight or had words, right? I mean the three of you used to be almost inseparable."

"We're fine. Everyone's been busy doing their own thing lately. But no . . . no problems. I don't know of any reason why I haven't spoken to her in the last couple of days other than the storm. Actually, I haven't spoken to Maureen in the last couple either. We've all sort of branched out with additional friends at Northridge and out of Northridge. Meeting new people is fun. You've said so yourself. So that's probably why, as I think about it."

"I haven't seen Phil lately either, but it's usually you girls who get us all together. He told me he's into his photography mode right now, so I told him to call when he's ready to go to the club and shoot some trap. I guess we're all a little out of touch."

"I'm glad the storm's finally over and that we missed the worst of it," said Shirley. "Maureen and I are going over to the clubhouse to see what's going on."

"What you really want to do is check on the gossip," said Chuck. "I'm not criticizing, because I'm curious myself. Can you believe it—the Weinberger's caught up in another murder. Maybe we need to think about ending our friendship with them. I don't want to be the next murder victim around here," and he made a face.

"That's awful," said Shirley. "We're friends, and they need our support. They don't need us making stupid jokes. I'm going. Do you want to join us?"

"No, I'm going to stay here and watch the news. I'm sure you'll fill me in when you get back. And I think we should go over to Phil and Judy's later. You know . . . let them know we're there for them. I'm sure Judy is crushed. Didn't you tell me she always felt Mary Rafferty was almost like a mother to her?"

"You're right there. Judy always talked about her strong feelings for Mary. Okay, I'm going to the clubhouse with Maureen. I don't think I'll be gone long. I'm sure no one will know very much, but maybe someone who volunteers at town hall or the police station will be around, and they might know something."

Shirley and Maureen wandered around the clubhouse. There were small groups gathered everywhere. There was so much to talk about—Hurricane Sandy and how it had luckily missed the Cape, friends and relatives in New York and New Jersey who had not been so lucky, damage from the rain and wind at Northridge, and of course—the big one—the murder of a resident and the robbery of her neighbor. Everyone was speculating. They made their way to the card room. Some people were attempting to play mahjong and others, canasta or bridge. Although the tables were set out for the games, talk and speculation were the real focus. Sandy noticed Maureen and Shirley first and called them over to the mahjong area.

"Hey you two. What's going on with your friend Judy? Everyone's talking about it. You probably know more than we do. Fill us in."

"Sandy," said Maureen while moving closer, "we just found out like everyone else, and we've hardly had a chance to talk to her. They're over at the police station now, so I'm sure we'll know more pretty soon. They're distraught of course. Mary was like a mother to Judy. Did you know she lost her mother a few years ago? Well when Mary moved in next door, they sort of hit it off." Maureen moved a little closer, took off her jacket and sat down. "We socialized with her a couple of times at Judy's house. Nice lady. I didn't connect with her like Judy did, but my mother's still alive, so maybe I didn't have Judy's needs. I remember Phil telling Ron that Mary didn't have any family or even friends other than those at Northridge. He said he thought it was strange not to have other connections." Shirley nudged Maureen. "What? I'm not saying anything bad. Well Phil told Ron he had offered to help Mary do an internet search, but she said it wasn't necessary because there was no one she cared to find. Her refusal seemed to bother Phil, according to Don, but Phil said it didn't bother Judy. That's all I know. What about you guys?"

Sandy said, "Everyone's sort of looking at everyone else because of Barbara Fisher, who works at the police station. You know . . . in exchange for a tax abatement. She walked over to the station this morning to see if she could help out, and she overheard an officer say that someone living here might have committed the murder. When Barbara told me that, I was shocked. Another murder here is bad enough, but if it was one of the residents, that would be unbelievable. I don't think anyone would have been out in that awful storm, so someone from here could have simply walked over without being seen."

Sandy was commanding everyone's attention, as she probably had been before Maureen and Shirley arrived. She was a fast talker who could string multiple sentences together without taking a breath.

"Before the two of you got here, we were trying to think of who in this community is the killer type," said

Sandy. "I know that's crazy, but if we all brainstorm maybe we can come up with an idea for the police. We know all the people here. The police don't. It might even be one of us," and she grinned while her friends groaned and shook their heads in disbelief.

Shirley spoke first. "Are you guys really planning to give the police a list of people who live here—people who you think could have killed Mary Rafferty and then robbed Judy's house? That's horrible if you are. What if your name was on some resident's list, and the police called you in, and you were innocent? Do you think you could continue to live here wondering who suggested your name? My God, that's like the McCarthy era of Communist hunting in this country, when innocent people were branded for no reason. I think you better think twice before you continue."

Smoke was emanating from Shirley, and Maureen stared at her in disbelief. "I'm sure Sandy and the girls don't plan on creating a list in the way you took it, Shirley. For heaven sakes, we all live here. We've known some of these people in Northridge for years. I'm sure it was some stranger who killed Mary. Let's not start swiping at one another."

"Well, maybe I overreacted a little, but let's be careful with what we say and what we repeat. I'm leaving Maureen. I told Chuck I wouldn't be gone too long. Are you coming?"

Without a word, Maureen followed Shirley out. As soon as they left the card room, everyone in Sandy's group started to talk at once.

"Boy Sandy, she sure chewed you out," said Pat. "But she's right. We don't want to make anyone's life miserable. We're all a little unnerved what with the storm, the murder, and then the robbery."

"Don't you start picking on me too. I didn't mean any harm. I'm as shocked as the next guy. But we live here.

This isn't some story on the evening news. This is our home, and I was only trying to help. I wasn't trying to start some gossip."

"You said the word gossip, not any of us," said Pat. "Actually, I'm getting a little uncomfortable here. I think I'll go home too. The rest of you can play three-handed mahjong. Remember, we learned how to do that last week when there were seven of us instead of eight."

With that, Pat picked up her mahjong card and handbag and walked away as the other girls stared in disbelief.

CHAPTER 10

Judy and Phil were escorted to a small interrogation room at the station. Judy, with Phil's help, told the detectives everything she could remember about Mary's diary entries. As a recorder captured their words, both detectives took notes for later reference. Occasionally one of them stopped and asked a question. The questions were meant to help Judy remember. It was difficult for her, and she often brushed away a tear. When she had related all she could remember, the detectives switched gears. Cotter asked if Mary had seemed upset or agitated recently, and Judy shook her head. Detective Partridge then asked about Mary's friends.

"Mary pretty much kept to herself," said Judy, "but she did have a few friends at Northridge. She liked to play cribbage on Tuesday evenings, and one of the new players started to pick her up because Mary didn't like to drive at night. I wouldn't say she was a loner," Judy said through a new batch of tears, "but she didn't seem to need very much. She liked to watch television, read, and play scrabble online. Mary loved her online scrabble game. She always tried to get me interested, and I did play online with her a few times, but it really wasn't for me. Mary said the best part was the people she met online from all over the world. She said it was really fun."

Cotter and Partridge thanked the Weinbergers and escorted them to the lobby. Then the detectives sat down with a fresh pot of coffee to review what they had learned and decide how they would proceed.

"This coffee is awful. It tastes like mud," said Partridge who sounded more than a little annoyed. "I think I'm going to buy one of those coffee pots that brew a single cup at a time. I can't think while drinking this sludge. So what do we know after talking to the Weinbergers?"

They threw ideas back and forth and reread all their notes. "Since the storm was predicted and residents on the Cape were advised by the police to stay at home, the perp could have walked to the Rafferty house," said Partridge. "The storm would have created a perfect cover. I say for now we focus on Northridge residents."

"We can't question everyone who lives at Northridge," said Cotter. "With over five hundred homes, I bet you're talking a thousand or so people to question."

"When did you hear me say we'd question everyone? Sometimes I can't believe you Cotter. How long have you been doing this work? Think man, think."

Cotter bit his tongue. He knew the guy didn't mean any harm, and he was fairly certain Partridge's abrasive edge was the result of his years as a New York detective, as well as his failed marriage. Actually, Cotter thought, Partridge had mellowed since he started dating the chief's sister, although he didn't talk about Cynthia very often and didn't like to be questioned about their relationship.

"Cotter, why don't you interview the members of that cribbage group," said Partridge. "That seems to be her only outside interest. Find out anything you can to establish a more complete profile, and let's go back and question the neighbors . . . did they see or hear anything." Partridge checked off items on his list. "I know Rinaldo and his team did that, but you follow up and do it again. Also, question neighbors about the break-in at the Weinbergers. You know, if anyone saw or heard anything no matter how small. We didn't have that piece before. Someone must know something. Someone had to have heard something. I'm going to check with forensics and see what they have. Our murderer wanted something from the victim and killed her while trying to get it. He also had to have known about her relationship with Judy Weinberger. Otherwise, why would he turn up there? The diaries appear to be the only items stolen, so the information we need has to be in something Mrs. Weinberger read. Now I believe more than ever that it was an inside job, inside Northridge."

Before heading home, Judy and Phil stopped at Siena for lunch. They ordered pizza, and Phil told Judy to order a glass of wine.

"I don't want wine," she said. "It makes me tired."

"I'm going to get a beer. We both need to relax a little."

"I hope we don't see anyone we know," she said. "I'm not in the mood to talk. I'm tired, and I'm talked out. I hope what I remembered from the diaries helps them find who did this disgusting thing."

"If you had listened to me in the first place…"

"Don't start with me again, Phil. You've made your point a million times. Drop it or I'll walk right out of here. I've had enough aggravation for a lifetime."

Judy checked the local paper when they got home. She immediately found what she was looking for, an article about Mary's murder. It was right there on the front page, but it was very brief . . .

MURDER AT GATED COMMUNITY

Investigators were on the scene yesterday of a grisly homicide in the Northridge Condominium Community in Marshland.

Mary Rafferty, 78, was found dead in her bathtub of multiple stab wounds. She was discovered by a neighbor who had entered the house to check on Rafferty during yesterday's storm that did so much damage in other states.

Local police are being assisted by the State Police Special Emergency Response Team. This is a team specially trained in searching for evidence.

Funeral arrangements are pending at present.

Anyone with information should contact the Marshland Police at 727-1717.

No further details were available at press time.

CHAPTER 11

Judy told Phil she was going to lie down. He never disturbed her when she napped because a nap meant she was really tired and needed to rest. Phil was a horrible snorer, and Judy often tossed at night, unable to block him out. But she never left to sleep on the sofa. She would simply cough or kick to make him stop. "What if he stopped breathing at night?" she told her kids when they suggested she sleep in the other bedroom. "I need to hear him if that ever happens. I need to be there if he needs me in the middle of the night." So she stopped complaining to them because she didn't want to hear them lecture her about the other bedroom. They were young. They were married, but they did not understand the fears that crept into a spouse's head as they both aged.

Judy closed the bedroom door, removed the bed covering, and reached for the rest of the diaries. She had not lied to Phil when he asked if she had finished reading them. She had told him the truth. She hadn't finished. And then they were stolen. What she had not told him or the detectives was that the thief had not found all the diaries. She had kept the unread ones hidden under her bed. She knew there would be hell to pay, but she did not want to think about that now. She wanted to finish them. She knew she could dream up an excuse later. She began to read . . .

Dear Diary,

    I never reached California. I landed in Arizona instead. My car broke down on Highway 89, not far from Flagstaff. Smitty kept telling me to take the car to a garage for a check-up because it wasn't a new car. I bought it used when I first moved to Vegas, and then, after meeting Smitty, I didn't use it that much. He always said if you have a car, you need to take care of it. I didn't listen. I guess I never listen to anyone, which is why my life is so screwed up. The mechanic said the work was going to be costly and suggested that I buy a new car, or at least a newer car. Something about driving around without changing the oil and the damage the gunk caused. So here I was in a new place without a car and without a friend. I was afraid to reach out to the ones in Vegas because I was afraid of the people who murdered Smitty. And I had left Miami too long ago to simply pick up the phone and call someone from there. My only choice was stay in Arizona, earn some money, buy a new car this time, something dependable, and then go to San Diego. Smitty always talked about visiting San Diego. He grew up there and always said he wanted to go back to visit and show me around . . .

    The people in Flagstaff seemed nice enough, so Mary decided to stay for a while. She got a job as a waitress, bought a good used car, and did some sightseeing. There had been little opportunity for sightseeing in her life. She had wanted to travel while she was living in Amsterdam, but Joey was always there to stop her. He had ruled her life, and she had been lucky to get away from him. She always wished she had seen more of that city, especially Anne Frank's house. Mary remembered reading *The Diary of Anne Frank*, and she regretted being so close and not having visited. She sometimes wondered what would have happened if she had been more assertive with Joey. He had always clamped down on her when she tried, and she had always been too much of a wimp to continue. That was until the last time, the time when she took everything and left. But those memories were from another life. She was no longer a naïve scared kid. She needed to take care of herself.

Mary enjoyed her work at the coffee shop and liked working the morning shift because it gave her time to explore. She especially loved the cacti with their beautiful flowers. A customer told her about one variety that looked like a person with arms. He explained that the saguaro cactus started to flower when it was around thirty years old and at seventy-five years old grew arms. He said a one hundred and fifty-year-old saguaro could be fifty feet tall and weigh about eight tons. That idea boggled her mind. Mary told customers that she liked to learn new things. She had been a poor student in high school, not like her older sister Brenda. Brenda had been quite a student—honor roll all the time and a joy to her parents.

Occasionally Mary thought about her family. Her parents would be in their late seventies if they were still alive. She wondered if her sister Brenda had gone on to college as she had always dreamt of doing. She wondered if Brenda had married and now had a family of her own. Mary had never tried to contact them, and they would have been unable to find her since she had changed her name to prevent that from happening. She knew what was done was done, and that idle daydreaming was simply idle daydreaming. She knew she needed to put those thoughts out of her mind.

The years moved by swiftly. Mary continued to work at the coffee shop, eventually moving into a managerial position at the Flagstaff location when the owner expanded into Sedona. She was a trusting woman and had never checked on Mary's background. Mary had changed her name from Sheila Nichols to Mary Richards to prevent those who killed Smitty from finding her. She had become quite proficient at name changes and the necessary paper work that went with them. She had learned from the best and probably could have sold her skills. Other women might have cashed in on that skill, but not Mary Richards. Mary Richards was simply a woman in her forties with no family, a made-up history of loved ones killed in a horrific accident, and the need for a quiet life. Of course there were men—men who wanted to know her better. But she had experienced enough of life with men who let her down, and she was not about to become involved again . . .

Dear Diary,

I was older now, and I'd learned a great deal about life and what matters. What mattered was peace of mind, and I had found that in Flagstaff. I could have married. I could have gone back to school to learn a profession. It would have paid better than managing a small coffee shop. And I could have gone on to San Diego as I had planned before fate brought me to Flagstaff. But I didn't do any of that. I stayed where I was. I stayed in Flagstaff until my late fifties . . .

"Mary, isn't your birthday next week? Let's celebrate. We could go to Sedona and stay at one of those nice bed and breakfasts or to the Grand Canyon and do some hiking and eat some good Mexican food or even to Vegas. What do you say?"

His name was Stephen, Stephen Murray. He owned the jewelry store next to the coffee shop and came in every day for lunch. At first he would only smile and thank her for his order. He was always polite, and he always left a small tip. Leaving a tip at a take-out coffee shop was not the standard practice for most customers, but Stephen always placed a dollar in the tip jar. Soon their conversations extended beyond a mere thank you or talk of the weather. Some of the help would tease her and say Stephen seemed to really like her. No one but Mary was surprised when he first asked her out on a date. Despite his persistence, Mary passed on the invitation.

"Thanks Stephen, but I've sworn off dating. Too many bad memories." He eventually won her over with his perseverance, and they would attend an occasional movie together and even have quiet dinners at some of the less trendy restaurants known only to the locals. One day he upped the ante and suggested a weekend together to celebrate her birthday.

"You never give up," she said.

"Well you're a lot of fun when you give a guy a chance," he said, while smiling at her affectionately. "I'd like more time to enjoy your company."

Mary grinned. "You think I'm a lot of fun? You should try living with me. I bet you'd change your mind in a minute."

They both laughed. "Come on," he said. "Give it a chance. It's your birthday, and you should do something special. You work too hard. Everyone agrees. So what do you say? We can go anywhere you want. We can even go to Vegas for the weekend. I remember you said you used to live there. I love to drive, and you could show me around. I don't really know much about the place. It would be fun."

"I'm tempted," she said while marveling at his determination. Everyone in town knew him, and everyone liked him. He was sincere, honest, and even pretty good-looking. Stephen had never been married. The reason had something to do with caring for his parents as well as never finding the right woman. "Let me think about it," she said. "It's been a long time since I lived in Vegas, but I really loved the energy of the place. I know I could show you around, and we could have fun. Give me a little time to think."

His face lit up, and he started to cheer. Her suggestion that she needed a little time to think about the offer was more than he had hoped for. Sure, they had always enjoyed one another's chatter when he came into the coffee shop, as well as during their occasional movie or dinner. He had even bought her small presents that she kept after protesting he shouldn't have, but this was different. She was actually thinking about going away with him. Stephen was hopeful. He did not know what it was about this woman that made him feel drawn to her. She was a little older than he was and quite attractive, although no one would describe her as beautiful. She rarely talked about herself or her life prior to coming to Flagstaff. All he knew was that she had lost her family in an accident and had arrived in Flagstaff because of car trouble while she was on her way to San Diego.

Stephen asked about her life before Flagstaff, but she never told him much beyond mentioning the family auto accident and her need to put it all behind her. He never pushed, knowing how difficult it was to talk about his own family situation. But now, now that his parents had both passed away, he wanted to have a life of his own. Maybe this woman, he thought, maybe this Mary Richards would turn out to be the special one.

Mary was nervous and excited at the same time. She had led a quiet life in Flagstaff for almost ten years. She really liked Stephen, but her life was peaceful and uncomplicated. If she agreed to a weekend away, she wondered if he would put more demands on her time. She was also worried about going to Vegas. She didn't want to put Stephen in any danger, although it had been almost ten years since Smitty's murder. She had never reached out to anyone in Vegas, so no one there knew where she was. She had changed her name and looked totally different now. Mary did not have to work hard at changing her appearance. She could not afford nail appointments, hair appointments, or beautiful clothes—all things that had made her look attractive in the past. She had learned to feel comfortable in jeans and a shirt. Life in Flagstaff was casual, and there was little difference between how she dressed at work and how she dressed when she and Stephen grabbed a movie or went to dinner.

The invitation aroused a desire for a taste of her old life. So she said, "Stephen I'd love to go to Vegas for the weekend. I can show you some great places, but I want us to get separate rooms, and I want to pay for my room. I don't want to take advantage of your offer, and you know my rules about getting serious."

"I'm just happy you agreed. Anything you want works for me. What if I get a room with two double beds? That way you won't feel pressured, and you won't have to spend any of your hard earned money. Please say yes."

"You drive a hard bargain. Okay, let's do it. Wait until I show you around the strip with all those big hotels and casinos. Of course I won't gamble, but I used to. It was a lot of fun. I'm so excited. When do you want to go?"

She let him hug her, and he was elated. "I'll get someone to cover my hours," he said, "and you do the same at the coffee shop. Let's shoot for the weekend of the nineteenth. How does that sound?"

"The nineteenth is only ten days away, but I'm sure I can get someone to cover," she said. "Everyone always says I should be better to myself, and they all know and love you. I know it will work. Oh Stephen, what a special way to spend my birthday. I love you for this surprise."

He let out a giant laugh. "Love me? Is that right. And all it took was an invitation for a Vegas weekend. I guess I haven't been very smart," and he laughed again even harder.

She blushed and said, "You know what I mean." Then she said, "Wow . . . I'm going to Vegas after all these years," and she hugged him.

Dear Diary,

We had so much fun in Vegas. Stephen was totally different from the other men I had known. But then I saw a familiar face, and I nearly fainted. I was staring at one of the guys Smitty had worked for. He looked straight at me and called me Sheila. I told him he was mistaken and my name wasn't Sheila, but he insisted. At that moment I knew we were in trouble. I was so stupid. I had been safe in Flagstaff. Why had I agreed to return to Vegas? It was horrible, and even now I'm having trouble writing about that day . . .

Stephen saw the expression on her face when they were confronted and suggested that they go to another restaurant. They left, and Stephen gave his ticket to the parking attendant. It all happened really fast after that. The guy followed them out of the restaurant, grabbed the ticket from the attendant's hand, and said they weren't going anywhere. Stephen tried to push him away and said, "What do you think you're doing? Be careful before someone gets hurt."

The guy said there's only one person here who's going to get hurt if you don't mind your own business, and he continued to call her Sheila. When Stephen stepped forward to move her out of the way, he was met with a punch to the groin. The punch caught him by surprise. He fell and hit his head on a cement step. The guy who had confronted her and punched Stephen ran off. The rest was awful. Stephen lost consciousness almost immediately and was rushed to the nearest hospital, but he never made it. He died on the way.

Dear Diary,

The police were wonderful. I said the incident was simply a matter of mistaken identity, and they didn't push the issue. I managed to go back to the hotel, get my things, and rent a car. I knew it wouldn't be long before the mob tracked me down. I knew I had to move quickly. I had always known in the back of my mind that something like this might happen. I knew they were afraid of what Smitty might have told me. So I drove back to Flagstaff in the middle of the night, gathered my belongings, and left without telling anyone what had happened. I'm sure my friends and everyone in the restaurant were shocked when I disappeared, but I had to disappear. I was afraid. I knew what they had done to Smitty. I knew what had happened to Stephen. I knew I could be next.

But where to go? I needed to get out of the Southwest. I decided a big city was probably the best place to disappear. I ditched the rental, bought a car, and drove to New York. I had lived there once and hoped to get a job waiting on tables without too many questions asked. I had disappeared before, and I knew I could do it again. This time I wouldn't be stupid. This time I really planned to keep to myself. Poor Stephen. First Smitty and now Stephen. I had lost two of the best things that had ever happened to me. I told myself I wasn't going to let it happen again. I knew my way around New York, and I knew how anonymous it could be. I prayed that my plan would work.

CHAPTER 12

Santiago had the diaries, and he started to search them for information that would put him on easy street. He wondered why the boss had not ripped them out of her hands all those years ago. Maybe they had seemed harmless to him since everyone had said her writing was probably therapy, like the therapy they gave crazies in the nut house. Santiago thought they had been too tolerant. She was a looker who brought in good money, and she was also smart. She saw everything and said nothing. Half the time people forgot she was there, and they would talk about issues that could have put all of them away. Then one day she had vanished, and the boss freaked. He offered a reward to anyone who would bring him her diaries and make her disappear. The boss said it was dangerous for all that information to be out there. Now he, Santiago, had them. And now she was dead. He searched for years hoping to both collect the reward and protect his own hide. The stakes were upped when quite by accident he saw a campaign billboard about the big boss. Damned if the boss hadn't cleaned up his act and become some kind of politician. Now Santiago was really determined to find her. He planned to blackmail the boss and end up with even more money in his pocket.

He had broken into her home under cover of the storm

and found her soaking in the bathtub. He had startled her, and she had screamed. He held a knife to her throat and told her to be quiet. She recognized him. He said he had been looking for her and her diaries for years. She refused to tell him where they were despite his repeated threats to hurt her if she didn't cooperate. She swore that she had not written anything in them that could cause a problem for him or the others. He didn't believe her. Frustrated by her refusal to hand them over, he had stabbed her repeatedly. He could still hear her screams. And then he had fled back into the storm. The wind was blowing the rain sideways, the visibility was close to zero, and it was pitch black with all the power out. He nearly tripped twice. He was sure no one had seen him, but he was freaked. She was dead, he had killed her, and he still did not have the diaries. Without those diaries, his blackmail get-rich-scheme was going nowhere.

The very next day he had taken another risk and broken into the home of her best friend, Judy Weinberger. Despite the police presence next door, he had easily slipped in by passing himself off as one of the workmen hired by Northridge to clean up after the storm. He was unbelievably lucky to find no one at home and found a pile of diaries on a table after first turning over some furniture and rifling through some drawers. They had always called him a loser, but who was a loser now, he thought. The diaries were finally in his hands, and he was sure he would find all sorts of incriminating information in them. He had taken a deep breath and smiled to himself. She had turned out to be pretty stupid for such a smart lady. He could smell the money.

With diaries in hand and the knife buried where no one would ever find it, he had taken off down Cape. The weather had turned beautiful, as it usually does after a storm, and he wished he had time to explore the beach.

Checking out changes to a beach after a storm had been a hobby of his since he was a kid in Florida. His grandfather was the one who had introduced him to the fun. They would collect shells brought in by the fury of the water, take loads of pictures, and maneuver through the deep rifts in the sand where the tide had surged. Although the Cape beaches were different, he knew he would still enjoy a sense of discovery, but the fun would have to wait. He had the diaries, and he needed to read them as soon as possible.

The thought of his rental had fueled a sense of calm as he drove down Cape. He knew the importance of not drawing attention to himself, so he observed the speed limit and slowly made his way down 6A. A guy he had met at a coffee shop told him 6A was a historical road that looked like old Cape Cod. He told Santiago to stay away from Route 28 because it was full of cheap motels and miniature golf courses with awful waterfalls and dinosaurs. The guy said they had built the things to attract families, but he couldn't understand people taking vacations with kids, since all he ever saw were screaming kids who always wanted more.

As Santiago drove through Barnstable, Yarmouth, Dennis, and Brewster, he wondered what his life might have been like if he had grown up in one of those towns. They were all so similar—town squares with clusters of stores and restaurants, white churches surrounded by picket fences, historical houses, and of course beautiful beaches. Santiago had grown up in Florida but in a crummy neighborhood full of crime. If anyone drove through his neighborhood, like he was now driving down Cape, they would have been stopped. No one drove through his hometown unless they belonged. Strangers always stuck out and usually were accosted by boys looking for a little excitement. Everyone in the neighborhood had family and friends in jail, and they knew that was where they would probably end up. There was no fear of the police, so confronting strangers who dared to drive into the neighborhood was a way to have a little fun.

He wondered why he was thinking about all that because what he could hardly wait to do was check out the crazy bitch's diaries. But first he wanted to get to the safety of his rental which was near Nauset Beach. And then the thought struck him . . . what if he drove to that beach and sat in his car. No one would probably be around to bother him at this time of year. It could be a perfect place to read, and he could even take a break and walk along the water's edge. He had heard that Nauset was a beautiful beach with long stretches of sand meant for taking quiet walks. There were sure to be large waves from the hurricane, and he had always loved to watch them come crashing onto the shore. The beach had a gigantic parking lot, and someone at the motel had told him tourists got there very early, like eight in the morning, to get a space. Santiago thought that was a little crazy and wished he was near the beaches of New Jersey, where the brunt of the hurricane hit. That would really be a blast. He heard on his car radio that police were keeping everyone away from the Jersey shore, and that some of those poor slobs had lost everything. But he knew he did not have to worry. He would soon be on easy street.

CHAPTER 13

Judy continued to read the diaries she had hidden under her bed, but started to skim them in an effort to finish as soon as possible. She knew she would be in trouble with Phil for hiding them and in trouble with Detectives Partridge and Cotter for not turning them over to the investigation. However, she did not know she was about to discover a truth that would change her life . . .

Dear Diary,

How did I manage to end up all alone in New York at my age? I'd certainly made a mess of my life. The money I earned as a waitress wasn't enough for New York, where everything is meant for people with big bucks. So I thought it might be time to go back to my roots—to my family, but I didn't know if anyone was still around who would even know me. I wasn't interested in finding friends—I wanted to find family. I didn't want to put them in danger, so I was cautious. I decided to simply observe them from a distance if I found them. That way, if someone was looking for me, they wouldn't be able to hurt my family . . .

CHAPTER 14

"Welcome back, Detective Cotter. Thought you got lost. Find out anything about the murder or the Weinberger break-in?" said Partridge.

"Not a damn thing on either," said Cotter. "As far as the break-in at the Weinberger place, it seems everyone was focused on the storm's damage and cleanup. So everything they saw was storm related. The landscape guys were all busy with chain saws, so that took care of what someone might have heard. They were clearing debris from everywhere—driveways, porches, decks, front steps, you name it. Because the Weinbergers had a big tree on top of their car, and because it was near the crime scene, it was one of the first areas cleaned. Our guy probably blended right in. So I don't think we'll get much from that angle."

"Crap," said Partridge. "What about that cribbage group?"

"Hold your horses and let me get my notes. Can't remember it all. Not a magician you know. I questioned a hell of a lot of people today. All of that takes time."

"So now you're telling me how much time it takes to question people," said Partridge. "Thanks for the education. Sometimes . . . ," and he emphasized sometimes.

"Alright, Mr. Sarcasm. Do you want to hear what I learned, or do you just want to stand there and needle me?"

"Needle you. Of course, needle you. A guy's got to have some fun. Lighten up." and Partridge laughed while poking Cotter in the ribs.

"Yeah, yeah. I'm light. Well it seems like there's sort of a revolving group who play cribbage. Sometimes they all show up, and sometimes only a few show up. It's a casual game, and I got a list of who usually plays from that woman Elsie Francheska. She's the one Mrs. Weinberger told us about. Nice lady. Well, this Elsie Francheska was pretty much of a mess when I talked to her. Couldn't tell me a great deal. Said if the Rafferty woman called, she would pick her up. Said they never sat together at the game because Rafferty was an experienced player and she was sort of new at the game. Asked her the usual questions about Rafferty's demeanor the past few weeks and if Rafferty ever seemed upset about anything. This Francheska woman said nothing stood out. Said they just talked about the game and chit-chatted about some of the players. She said she couldn't think of anything special. Thanked her for the other names and plan on contacting them during the next couple of days. So, I've nothing so far. Sorry."

"Seems like no one around here knows squat," said Partridge. "Keep working on that cribbage angle."

"You have anything?" said Cotter.

"I'm still working on names and places the Weinberger woman remembered from reading those diaries," said Partridge. "Boy this job continues to amaze me. Go figure, some old lady with no apparent connections outside of Northridge turns out to have a bunch of aliases and a background of crime and prostitution. Damn . . . wish we had those diaries."

"Sounded like Weinberger's husband was ready to blow he was so mad at her for not turning the diaries over immediately," said Cotter. "Shame he didn't get his way.

Think she told us everything? Maybe she held something back like she did with the Jerry Smith murder investigation."

"Good for you, Cotter. Maybe you do have some potential. I remember that now. But when we were investigating the Jerry Smith death, she was trying to keep a secret from her husband. Not sure what she'd be hiding in this investigation."

"What about forensics and DNA?" said Cotter still beaming from Partridge's left-handed compliment. "Maybe we'll be lucky and find that the guy nicked himself or something. We need a break. It only happened yesterday, but you know the folks over at Northridge. They'll be down the chief's back pretty soon, and then he'll be on our case. Hope it won't be one of those unsolvable crimes. Hate to think someone could get away with both a murder and a robbery."

"Are you shitting me?" said Partridge. "We haven't even scratched the surface and already you're thinking the worst. There's lots to investigate. Just do your work, and let me worry about the chief and the big picture."

"Right boss. Anything you say boss. What's next boss? Glad you know everything, boss, because you're the big shot New York cop."

"Alright. Alright. Got the picture," said Partridge. "I did get some stuff. Was able to trace the name Mary Rafferty back to Miami but can't find a thing on her before age eighteen or thereabouts. Seems she was involved back then with a minor gangster who free-lanced as a pimp. She got picked up several times for prostitution, minor theft, and the likes. Then it seems she worked as a high-end escort making big money while still sticking with this small time gangster who eventually moves her to Amsterdam, of all places. Now the trail gets interesting. Seems this pimp gets jailed over there for causing a ruckus when she cleans him out, and she supposedly leaves the country. We can't find anything else about her until she turns up here. Working the pimp angle now."

"What about forensics?" said Cotter. "Anything come in about that?"

"Yah, we might be lucky there," said Partridge. "They have a couple of fingerprints and part of a footprint found on the rug in the living room. They also found a couple of hairs that don't check out as belonging to the victim. The hairs were found in the bathroom, so we might get some additional DNA from there. I'm going back to talk with Mrs. Weinberger. I think she's our best bet. There's a reason Rafferty wrote those diaries."

Judy finished the last of the diaries and shook her head in confusion. Could Mary be trying to tell her something? Could these last entries contain hidden messages? They seemed so different from the earlier ones. The new entries were all about trivial things, and Judy felt there had to be an explanation.

And then her thoughts jumped to Phil in the other room. She had told him that she wanted to take a nap. Now, if she shared her suspicions with him, he would go nuts because she was not napping, was hiding the fact that there were additional diaries, and was misleading the police. She started to cry but quickly realized she had to pull herself together, stand up to Phil, and contact Detective Partridge. She couldn't figure this out herself. She needed help. She owed it to Mary. With those thoughts in mind, she opened the bedroom door.

"You feeling better?" said Phil. You were in there for quite a while.

"I'm fine," she said, "but . . . but there's something I want to tell you. Promise you won't yell. Just listen without interrupting. Promise?" She went over to where Phil was sitting, looked straight at him and said, "I mean it. Promise. I don't know how I'm going to get through this if you yell."

"What are you talking about? What's going on?"

"You didn't say promise. As soon as you promise, I'll tell you."

"Okay, I promise. Now tell me."

"It's about the diaries. There were more, and I finished reading them when you thought I was napping."

"What the hell is wrong with you Judy? For God's sake! What else have you lied about? What else are you hiding?"

"You're yelling. You promised you wouldn't yell."

"Well I lied. You aren't the only one who can lie you know. What do you think of them apples? I need to yell. I need to know why you can't leave well enough alone like a normal person. A normal person would have immediately turned all the damn diaries over to the police and let them do their work. But no, you need to play detective. Maybe we should send you to the Police Academy, and then you can get a job here in town solving all the crimes involving your friends. First it's Jerry Smith. Now it's Mary Rafferty. Who's it going to be next? I'm sick and tired of all this involvement in my life. I want it to stop. I mean it. Now!"

"Are you finished? I knew you'd act like a jerk. I knew you couldn't listen without yelling and lecturing. Do you want me to share, or should I just call Detective Partridge? Actually, I'm not telling you another thing. You'll only go crazy. I'm calling him right now, and you can find out what I discovered when I tell him." And she stormed back into the bedroom and slammed the door.

Partridge and Cotter were close by and arrived within a few minutes.

"Mrs. Weinberger, thank you for calling us. We hoped you'd have additional information."

"Yah, right," snickered Phil.

"Excuse me Mr. Weinberger," said Detective Partridge. "I don't understand. May we sit down?"

"Oh you'll understand soon enough, won't he Judy?" And Phil snickered for a second time.

"Now Mrs. Weinberger," said Detective Partridge raising an eyebrow as he glanced at Phil, "please tell us what you remembered."

"Well, it's not quite what I remembered," and she cleared her throat several times and grimaced.

"For God sakes Judy, blurt it out—enough clearing of the throat."

"Mr. and Mrs. Weinberger," smiled Partridge glancing from one to the other, "if this is a bad time for the two of you . . . "

"No, I think this is a perfect time," said Phil. "I think this nonsense has gone on long enough. Spit it out Judy before I tell them myself."

"Alright you two," said Cotter. "If this is a family disagreement, it's probably inappropriate for the two of us to be here."

"No, no," groaned Judy. "You need to stay. You see I wasn't totally truthful about Mary's diaries. There were more. There were some I hadn't read, and I hid those under my bed so I could finish them. The diaries on the table—the ones that were stolen—I had already read those. I didn't think it would end up like this. I just wanted to read everything Mary had written."

"You never think," said Phil. "That's your problem."

"Mr. Weinberger," interrupted Partridge before Phil had a chance to say anything further, "I think we need to hear what your wife has to say. Mrs. Weinberger, do you think it would help if you came down to the station to discuss this in private?"

"Alright, alright," stammered Phil. "I'll listen without

commenting."

"Mrs. Weinberger," smiled Cotter, "it's your call."

"I'd just as soon stay here as long as there are no interruptions from my husband," and she glanced in his direction. "I know he's angry, and I know I should have given you all the diaries, but I thought I was following Mary's wishes. In her letter she asked me to read the diaries and then give them to the police or destroy them. Mary said it was my choice. She said to read them from the beginning because I would understand everything that way. So that was what I was doing. I never intended to keep evidence from the police. I know I was wrong, and I'm really sorry."

"Please start from the beginning," said Partridge. "And Mrs. Weinberger, when we finish here, you need to give us that letter, the rest of the diaries, the box that the diaries came in, and anything else that was in the box Mrs. Rafferty gave you."

"Absolutely," said Judy. "I just want you to find Mary's killer and the person who stole her diaries from our house. Thank God they didn't get everything. I bet they saw Mary's diaries on the living room table and didn't think there'd be more. Maybe it's a good thing the rest were hidden under my bed," and she looked sheepishly at Phil.

Then Judy said, "I think Mary might have hidden a message in her last few entries."

"Oh," said Cotter while quickly glancing at Partridge. "What makes you think there might be a hidden message?"

"Well, Phil and I read Mary's most recent entries together. We thought she might have been worried about something and written about it in her diary, but neither of us felt we had read anything of importance. But now, as I think about the earlier entries—the ones where she wrote about her life and her regrets—the most recent ones seem totally different. I mean they're just full of everyday stuff.

For instance, she wrote about our Scrabble games. She loved the game, and I would go over and play with her when Phil was watching a Red Sox game. Why would she write about Scrabble? And she also wrote about her cribbage games, and our shopping trips, and even the weather. Why would she do that? It doesn't make any sense."

"We'll keep what you told us in mind Mrs. Weinberger," said Partridge. "I hope you've told us the whole story now and you aren't keeping anything else back. We have a murderer out there, and we need every bit of information if we're going to find him."

"You have every right to ask me that question, but I swear I've told you everything. Please believe me."

"Mrs. Weinberger," said Cotter, "as we told you earlier, withholding information is a serious offense. Please don't do anything else that might further jeopardize your situation."

"Should I get a lawyer?" Judy asked and started to cry.

"That won't be necessary," said Partridge, "but call us immediately if you remember more of what you read in those diaries. Now if you'll excuse us," and both detectives headed for the door.

"I'll show you out," said Phil. When he came back into the room, he glanced at Judy and shook his head.

"Don't you dare say anything," she said and went into the bedroom and shut the door.

"What's wrong with that woman?" shouted Yablonski. "Doesn't she know she's with-holding information and evidence from a murder investigation. You should throw the book at her, or better yet, get her the hell out of our town. Who does she think she is?"

"You're a hundred percent correct, and we're just as frustrated," said Partridge.

"How about evidence from the scene—what's the latest?" asked Yaablonski.

Cotter brought the chief up-to-date on the forensic report while Partridge excused himself and left with the box of evidence from Mrs. Weinberger.

Partridge placed the victim's letter as well as the remaining diaries on the table and reached into the box to make sure he had everything. Much to his surprise, he found a small brown envelope taped to the bottom. When Partridge emptied the envelope, a small key fell onto the table. Cotter came in as Partridge was puzzling over the key and envelope.

"Any surprises?"

"Yup," smiled Partridge, and he held up the key. "It seems Mrs. Weinberger missed something. Any idea what this might open?"

Cotter took the key and turned it over in his hand. "Looks like the key to my safe-deposit box. The wife and I got one of those a few days ago. With a big storm predicted and the possibility of wide-spread damage, she talked me into getting our important papers into a safe location. We went to Cape Cod 5 a few days ago and took out one of their safe-deposit boxes. I think our key has a number or something on it. Not sure. The wife's got it someplace. Only saw the key once or twice, but this here sure looks like one of those keys. What was your guess?"

"I didn't have a clue about the key. I'm not lucky enough to have a wife who pushes me to make smart moves, so I don't have one of those boxes. A safe-deposit box . . . interesting. I think I'll call Mrs. Weinberger, tell her what we found, and see what she thinks. Maybe we'll luck out here," he said half to himself. The phone rang and Mrs. Weinberger answered. Partridge told her about the key and Cotter's thought that it might open a safe-deposit box.

"I forgot all about that," she said. "Do you think it

might help you find out who killed Mary?"

"Mrs. Weinberger," said Partridge while giving Cotter a thumbs up, "please tell me everything you know about Mary's, I mean Mrs. Rafferty's use of a safe-deposit box. Do you know what's in it and what bank the key was issued from? Any information could help move us closer to the identity of her killer."

"It was taken out at the Cape Cod Savings Bank in Falmouth," said Judy. "You know, the one next to Headlines. That's where I get my hair cut, and that was where I took Mary when she wanted to get her hair cut. She didn't go very often. She liked to wear her hair pulled back into a bun. I wish you had known her. She was quite striking for a woman of her age. When she needed it cut, she'd always come with me. Well this one day, maybe a couple of months ago or so, she asked if we could go to the bank after we finished having our hair cut. She said she wanted to get a box for some of her papers. I'm so lame— how could I have forgotten all about that? Well we went next door to the bank, she filled out the paper work, and then she put some items in a small safe-deposit box."

"Mrs. Weinberger," said Partridge, "did you co-sign for her? Do you also have a key?"

"I think it's in my jewelry box. I threw it in there when I came home from the bank. Phil says I'm always misplacing stuff, but I think he loses more than I do. Well anyway, I put it in my jewelry box for safe keeping. Gosh I look in there every day, but I never thought of the key and the box. I'm sorry Detective. I'm just a mess over this. Do you want me to bring you the key?"

"Why don't you meet us at the bank in Falmouth first thing in the morning—say about ten," said Partridge. "If we had your key, we wouldn't have to get a court order and that would speed up the process. And, Mrs. Weinberger, I hope this is the last of the surprises because it's becoming a problem. Try to think if there's anything else, no matter how small, and we'll see you in the morning."

"I'm sorry," she said sounding like she was about to cry. "I promise," and she hung up the phone. Judy decided not to tell Phil about the key. She had had enough of his put downs, not that she hadn't deserved his scorn. It was all becoming too much for her—the storm, the murder, the robbery, Phil's yelling. What she wanted was to sit quietly and try and remember everything she had read in Mary's diaries and everything about that safe-deposit box. She wondered how she could she have forgotten all about it. She tried to remember if Mary had sounded concerned when she said she needed the box.

Judy wished she was like the people she had heard interviewed on television the previous week. They could remember any day, even years back, as if that day had just happened. But she did not have that ability and was having trouble remembering anything.

She agreed to meet the detectives at the bank the next morning because she did not want them at the house again. Her plan was to tell Phil she needed tennis socks from Marshalls and then drive to the bank instead. She hoped to pull it off, but the down side of being married for so many years was not being able to hide anything. Somehow Phil always caught on. Realizing the probable futility of her plan, Judy decided to tell him about the detective's phone call. Maybe he would even remember something she had forgotten.

She heard the garage door open and noticed a bag in Phil's hand as he came into the kitchen. "I didn't know you went out," she said. "Why didn't you tell me?"

"I did, but you probably never heard because you were mad at me and holed up in the bedroom. Have you calmed down?"

She chose to ignore him, nodded, and asked if he saw

anyone. That last question was standard whenever either of them went out alone.

"No, just stopped at the hardware store for some light-bulbs and masking tape. I need to fix the light in the basement near my workbench."

"I got another call from the detectives while you were out." Judy tried to sound as casual as possible.

"Oh?"

"It seems they found a key in the box that held the diaries. It was in a small envelope taped to the bottom. I never saw it. I guess I was focusing on all those diaries. Detective Partridge said it was sort of stuck under the bottom flap. He said he and Detective Cotter thought it might be a safe deposit key. I told them I remember taking Mary to get a safe-deposit box one day after we had our hair cut in Falmouth. Do you remember me telling you anything about it? I can't seem to remember very many details."

"I do remember," he said. "I remember telling you to put the key in a safe place. Do you have it?"

"Yes," she said and held up the key. "I put it in my jewelry box and forgot all about it. Wouldn't it be wonderful if something in that safe-deposit box sheds light on who killed Mary? I can't remember what she placed in it other than some papers, but I wasn't paying much attention. The detectives want me to meet them at the bank tomorrow morning around ten."

"I'll go with you. Driving to Falmouth might be tricky if some traffic lights are still out. I guess Mary's papers were important to her, and she was afraid of losing them," said Phil. "Otherwise, why would she take out a box at the bank? Remember, before I got our safe, we had a box at the bank. I even remember as a kid going to the bank with my mother and seeing the bank vault with all those brass boxes. It always seemed like such a secret place to me."

CHAPTER 15

He searched through the diaries for quite a while. There was a ton of damaging information about him and others if the police ever got to read them, but not the information he needed in order to collect his big reward. "Christ," he mumbled. He knew it had to be in there somewhere. Suddenly he heard a car drive up and stop. He wondered who would be out at the beach in this weather. When he looked up, he saw an Orleans police cruiser.

"How you doing sir?" the officer said. "Kind a cold to be sitting out here in the beach parking lot don't you think?"

The officer looked like a young kid, and he hoped the guy stopped because he was bored to death checking all the beach parking lots. "You're right there, officer," he said. "Had a little squabble with the girlfriend and thought I'd come out here to cool down a bit. No pun intended," and he laughed. "Love this place in the summer. Find it relaxes me. Hoped it might have the same effect now. Brought some stuff to do. You know, to try and catch up on work."

"Good luck," the officer said, "and hope it works out with the girlfriend. They can get a little crazed at times. You're probably smart cooling down away from her and letting her do the same," and then the officer drove off.

He went back to the diaries. He knew it had to be

there. She always wrote everything down. The thought that she had disappeared with information about him and the others had been hanging over his head for years. If someone else ever found the information, he knew they could blackmail him or worse. He had done his time for other crimes, and he never wanted to go back. Those years had been hell. He had worked hard after prison to keep his nose clean, but he never forgot the bitch and his dream of reward money. He always swore he would somehow track her down.

And then he had found her. It had taken him years, and it was crazy how it happened. He had been playing Scrabble on the internet and given himself the name of Lover Man. Occasionally he had even come across the name of someone he remembered playing with during a previous game. One of the people he kept running into online was named Cutie Pie, and he remembered that the bitch he had been tracking for years sometimes went by that name. Although it was crazy to think that this person could be the Cutie Pie he had known, he decided to play multiple games with her whenever she was online. Soon they were meeting and chatting online in one of the Scrabble rooms and playing extended sessions.

He learned that she had lived in Las Vegas as a young woman and was now retired and living in Massachusetts. He had been positive she was the right woman, and he had been more determined then ever to find her. She wasn't careful about the information she revealed, and he was able to narrow his search. She obviously had little knowledge of the dangers out on the internet. Cutie Pie had told him several things about herself. He had been astounded at the wealth of knowledge he was able to accumulate in a short time—Cape Cod, an upper Cape location, a gated retirement community, a clubhouse, a golf course. She even told him she had been born in Florida and had lived all over the country including Europe. He wondered how she had been so smart when she was young and how she could have become so careless and unaware.

And then he was face to face with her. He hadn't planned on killing her. He had only wanted to scare her and get the damn diaries. He had been sure she would crumble, but that naïve scrabble player was still the mean old bitch of years ago. She had laughed at him and refused to turn them over. She said he'd never find them. He had lost his temper, and then in a minute it was over, and now he was in a parking lot reading her diaries. He had torn her house apart looking for them, but they were nowhere to be found. He had been told a neighbor was her closest friend, and he had taken a risk and broken into her house and found them in clear sight. But he wasn't finding what he needed in the diaries. He wondered if there were more. He was positive that what he was looking for had to be somewhere. He had known her too well. She wrote everything down. It was like her sickness. If he was going to score big, he needed to find that information. "Damn her," he whispered.

CHAPTER 16

The phone rang and Partridge answered.

"Hello, is this Detective Partridge? My name is Max Alberts, and I live over at Northridge. Do you remember me? You were helping Judy Weinberger and me figure out who's been stealing items from our clubhouse. I know you've been busy what with the murder of poor Mrs. Rafferty and the robbery at Mrs. Weinberger's place, but I thought you should know there's more missing from our clubhouse. Everyone here is really upset and worried."

"Of course I remember you, and I haven't forgotten about the problem over there. We did have some information from an officer down Cape in Orleans. Actually I think it was a few days before the storm. We had sent out a list of your missing items to second-hand stores and the such as well as other police departments Cape wide hoping we might get lucky. It's buried here on my desk. What do you say I take a look and call you back."

"Thank you, that would be great. As I said, we're all upset here, and solving a small thing like this would help the community. And one more thing . . . I know you can't really tell me anything, but Mrs. Rafferty was such a nice lady—kept to herself most of the time you know. She was lucky to have Judy, I mean Mrs. Weinberger, as a good friend. Do you have any leads? People here can't think about anything else. They're scared. We're all a little past our prime, and it doesn't take much to spook us. And a murder, God, I can't believe a second murder here at Northridge. We all moved here thinking it would be safe— you know security at the gate and all. I guess nothing in this world is completely safe anymore."

"I hear what you're saying," said Partridge. "Sorry I can't tell you anything about the murder investigation, but I'll call you back with that other information. And try not to worry. We have several good leads that we're working on."

"I couldn't help overhearing your conversation," said Cotter. "I remember you getting something about that from a detective down in Orleans. Those poor people over at Northridge. They must be going crazy with worry. You'll probably have to go over there and meet with them like you did for the Jerry Smith murder. Boy, if my folks lived over there, I think I'd suggest that they move. It's not often we have murders in this town, and then, within a year, two in the same community. I thought lightening didn't strike twice in the same place."

With Cotter's help, it didn't take Partridge long to find the memo. It was something about a vase and a painting that had turned up in one of the second-hand stores. It referred them to a Detective Rathbare in Orleans. Partridge called him, and Rathbare answered on the first ring.

"Sure I remember you," he said. "We spoke a few days ago—right before the storm. Hey, how'd you folks make out up there? Any storm surges? We had some damage on Nausett, but we were lucky, luckier than the poor saps in Jersey. Hear you've got a big murder investigation going on up there. Any solid leads?"

"You know how it goes," said Partridge. "Loads of leads and nothing pans out. But it's early. Actually I'm following up on another issue in the same community. Hear you got word of an incident possibly involving stolen merchandise that might match up to two items stolen from here."

"Yah, yah, right. Well, this woman calls us a week or so ago. Says she owns the resale down on Route 28 in the same shopping center as Guapos. You like real good Mexican cuisine, that's the place to go. Well, she said this guy comes in, never saw him before, and says he has some stuff to sell. Then he takes a vase and a painting out of a big bag. She described the bag like from Marshalls. So the woman tells him they work on consignment, and they could certainly take his two items. He tells her he's a tourist in the area for just a few days and needs some cash. She explains how she can take his information, give him a receipt, and send him a check when the items sell. The guy says no good, just give me whatever you think they're worth. When she said she couldn't give him any money right at the moment, he got verbally abusive and left. She said he was parked out front, and she got his license. She said later that day she remembered a notice about some stolen items from up your way and wondered about the painting."

"Sure wish you had more for us," Partridge said, "but we'll take what we can get I guess."

"We'll keep our eyes and ears peeled down here, but right now that's all we've got. Hope it helps some, and listen—good luck with that murder investigation. Hear it's the same location as the murder you had last year. What are you folks doing up there? Don't send any of your big city crime down to us," and he hung up.

Partridge repeated the gist of Rathbare's conversation to Cotter.

"I haven't heard of any new break-ins at Northridge other than the one at the Weinbergers," Cotter said. "Have you?"

"Nope," said Partridge. "My guess is it's someone who lives over there, is visiting there, or works there. I'm willing to bet the guy who tried to unload those items was probably the fence. Just what we need—more problems over at Northridge."

"Not to change the subject," said Cotter, "but how's it going with you and the chief's sister? The wife said she saw the two of you over at the Commons on Sunday. And Rogers over at the bank said the two of you were in there on Friday. You're getting to be quite the couple," and Cotter grinned.

"Wipe that stupid grin off your face," said Partridge. "Yah, we've been spending a lot of time together. We seem to really get along well, if you and the rest of the world must know. She's easy to be with, she listens to my stories, and she doesn't make snide remarks like Cindy, my ex."

"Are you in contact with the first Mrs.?" asked Cotter.

"Nah, Cindy sort of disappeared off the face of the earth. We never should have married. We had nothing in common, and she never supported anything I did. Hell, being married to her was like being single. It's funny . . . I'm not married, yet with Cynthia I feel more married than I ever did with Cindy."

"Would you ever marry again?" said Cotter.

"What's this, twenty questions? Actually it's none of your damn business. But I know you won't stop bugging me, so I'll tell you. The answer is—I don't know. Things are good with the two of us. It's easy, and I don't want to jinx what we've got. So there. Now enough about me. How about we grab a coffee over at Panera?"

CHAPTER 17

She washed her face, put on lipstick, and whispered, "You're getting old babe, but you still look pretty good." She usually wore lots of makeup, but most people on the Cape seemed to wear very little. She could deal with an adjustment in the makeup department for a while, but she was itching for a new piece of jewelry. She had not lifted a thing since arriving on the Cape. The local stores were never crowded enough, and the sales people watched everyone too closely. She had heard good things about Copley Place in Boston, so that was her destination today. It was like a disease. She had been successful for decades swiping jewelry, wearing it for a while, and then selling it to a fence. Her usual method was to tell the manager or salesman that all her jewelry had been stolen, and she wanted to replace some items with the $25,000 insurance check she had just received. It was pretty easy to admire and try on several pieces and then swipe something small like a ring. She was good. It had worked countless times, and she was rarely caught. She had served some jail time but was usually put on probation. She loved the challenge and of course the jewels. He said he would take her. She wasn't afraid of driving into Boston herself, but she wanted company for the long ride.

"I'll be by about eleven," he said, "so call me in at the gate. No one to recognize me now." Before the murder, they always met off Cape to do their errands. It was a pain, but they knew they had to be careful. He had planned this for a long time, ever since he spotted her on that Scrabble site. And now he was almost finished except for one fact— he still had not found the entries that would put him on easy street.

He had been irritable on the phone, so she was a little nervous. She knew how easily he could fly off the handle and hoped he wouldn't be in an ugly mood when he picked her up.

CHAPTER 18

Partridge and Cotter arranged to meet Judy at the bank. She asked Phil to go with her, and she was up early in anticipation. Selecting the right outfit to wear was often a challenge, and she hoped it wouldn't be a problem this morning. Her closet was full of clothes, but she quickly became frustrated when she decided her new tight jeans that cost a fortune didn't quite go with the top she wanted to wear. She changed the jeans, but she still wasn't happy. Sometimes it took three tries to get dressed, and it drove Phil crazy.

He walked into the bedroom to see if she was ready. "Don't start this again," he groaned when he saw clothes all over the bed. "Are you going to try on everything in your closet before we leave the house? For God sakes Judy, I think you've got a sickness. You come home with bags every day, and then the next day you return most of what you've bought. You've got to stop this nonsense. You're fine. You're not going to the opera you know. You're going to meet them at the bank. Now hurry up so we're not late; they're already pissed at you. It's bad enough we're late every time we go out with our friends."

"Are you finished?" she said. "You always have a comment. It's amazing. I know what I'm doing. I'll be ready in a minute, and I won't embarrass you by being late. So cool your heels."

The detectives were at the bank when Judy and Phil arrived. Phil glared at Judy but didn't say a word.

"I hope we didn't keep you waiting," Judy said. "I was a little anxious thinking about what might be in the vault, so I was slow getting dressed." She tried not to glance at Phil but caught a brief glimpse of him rolling his eyes.

Cotter answered while smiling at her. "Don't worry. It's not a problem. We just got here ourselves. By the way, you'll be happy to hear that we got a call from Orleans about a couple of items that might have come from your clubhouse. I know you and Max Alberts have been working with us to find out who's been stealing your stuff. Seems someone down in Orleans tried to pawn both a painting and a vase. When the clerk said their store didn't give cash until an item was sold, the guy became verbal. The clerk took down the guy's plate number and called the police. They thought the items could be from Northridge. We'll check with the consignment shop for more details, but we thought we'd tell you because we know how hard you and Mr. Alberts have been working to solve the case. In fact, he called us yesterday to ask if we had any new information and to tell us how anxious the community is at the present time given the murder, your robbery, and the missing items from the clubhouse."

"Thank you for telling me," said Judy. "I still can't believe Mary's gone. I just want to know why someone killed her."

"We understand," said Partridge. "Now let's see what's in this safe-deposit box. Mrs. Weinberger, are you ready? Do you have the key?"

"I guess I'm ready," she said, "and the key is right here in my bag."

"Good," said Partridge. "Now the bank can let us in and we can both go over what we find."

Judy's hand shook visibly as she gave the key to Detective Partridge. "I've been a mess since Mary's murder," she said. "Maybe something we find will shed light on who killed her and why."

There were two items in the box—a diary like the ones that Judy had been reading and a letter addressed to her. Partridge took the diary and handed the letter to Judy.

"This letter is addressed to you Mrs. Weinberger, but given the circumstances, I think it'd be best if you read it here in the bank and then turned it over to Detective Cotter and myself."

Judy said she understood. They left the vault to join Detective Cotter and Phil—both of whom had been waiting in the bank's conference room. Judy opened the letter and planned to quickly scan it before sharing the contents with Phil and then the detectives.

"Judy, what's wrong?" said Phil. "You're white as a ghost. What's in Mary's letter that's so upsetting?"

"Oh my God Phil. Oh my God! Oh my God!"

"You've said that three times now. Talk to me. Breathe! What does it say?"

Unable to explain, Judy handed the letter to Phil who read it quickly before spitting out his own words of amazement. "She's got to be kidding. Is this true Judy? Are her facts accurate?"

All Judy could manage was a positive nod of her head and another oh my God.

"Mr. Weinberger," Partridge said, "if you don't mind, we need to take the letter addressed to your wife as evidence. And Mrs. Weinberger, obviously something in Mrs. Rafferty's letter shocked you. You need to share that with us."

"Phil, you tell them. I can't. I can't believe this."

"Detectives, what my wife and I just learned from reading this letter is very personal," said Phil, " and quite a shock to Judy as you can see. I'd like a minute with my wife, and then I'm sure we'll both be able to talk to you." With that, he put his arm around Judy and said, "Honey, do you need some water? You still look white as a ghost."

"No problem," said Partridge. "You can come down to the station later today to give us the letter. We understand it's very personal which is obviously why it was addressed to your wife. And Mrs. Weinberger, don't let us down. We're going way out on a limb here. We should be taking the letter, but we understand your need for more time to absorb its contents. Mr. and Mrs. Weinberger, don't forget. Later today at the station, please. We'll be expecting you."

Partridge and Cotter left Mr. and Mrs. Weinberger and headed back to the station. "What was that all about?" said Cotter.

"Damned if I know, but she certainly was spooked. Would loved to have taken the letter with us, but she seemed like she needed more time with it. Besides, it was legally hers. Her name was on the safe deposit papers, and she had the second key. Hope I didn't make a mistake giving her a few hours to absorb everything it said but didn't want to discuss a court order if she grumbled about turning it over. I thought letting her think we could have taken it but we let her hold it for a while was the best way to go."

"You're quite a guy," said Cotter sounding somewhat sarcastic. "You sure know your stuff being from the city and all," and he emphasized city.

"What's your problem," said Partridge, "and what's with the attitude? Fight with the wife today or is this an example of your usual jealousy? We've been partners for a while, and when you're in a shitty mood, your small cop envy comes roaring out. So stash it, okay. I've got a lot on my plate too, but I'm not taking it out on you. Grow up!" With that he gave Cotter the cold shoulder and turned his attention to the road as they headed back to the station.

Yablonski met them as they entered the station. "Been looking for you guys. Just got that DNA report on your case. No luck. Not a damn match in the whole system. It stinks, but that doesn't mean your guy's clean. He could've been convicted around the time the law took effect and been missed during the rush to collect DNA from everyone. That's one good avenue down the toilet, so the two of you better have something. I've got those people over at Northridge crawling up my ass wanting an update. You'd think they'd give us at least a week. Since it's your baby, you can set up the meeting. I've enough headaches, what with the mess from the storm and the press on my back wanting the lowdown on this case. Well, do you have a lead? You're never around when I want you guys, so it better be because you're working on a lead."

"Look who's got the attitude now," whispered Partridge just below Yablonski's hearing level.

"Did you say something?" said Yablonski. "I was up all last night with this damn cold. Think it's even affected my hearing. The wife says I never listen to her which is why I usually don't hear her. But you know how it is with wives, or at least you do, Cotter. Got to turn them off once in a while if you want some peace and quiet. Now get to work you two and bring me something. I need to be able to say more than . . . we're working on a lot of leads, but at this time I'm not at liberty to reveal anything in fear of jeopardizing the case. You know, the usual crap. So get moving. You do have something positive to move on besides a bunch of dead ends I hope."

"How about we meet with you later on today and fill you in." said Partridge. "We've new information but haven't had a chance to digest it yet. Does that work,

Chief?"

"Yeah, it works. Just move on the damn thing. I'm getting too old for all this media crap."

"You bet, Chief," said Cotter, and the two detectives headed to their office.

"Let's look at this new diary," said Partridge, "that's if we're still talking to one another," and he laughed. "There had to be a reason that the Rafferty woman put this one in a safe-deposit box rather than giving it to Mrs. Weinberger with the others. Strange woman, this Mrs. Rafferty. On the surface she's your ordinary senior citizen, but then we find out about call girls, escorts, and prostitutes. The more I'm in this business, the more I just shake my head."

Both Partridge and Cotter looked through the diary, but nothing jumped out at them except the strangeness of the entries considering it went into a safe-deposit box rather than into the group entrusted to Judy Weinberger.

"It's exactly what Mrs. Weinberger said about the last few diaries," said Cotter. "Rafferty just goes on about her cribbage games, her scrabble games, and her everyday life. I don't get it. No one spends money on a safety deposit box and then puts a diary of everyday activities into it."

They were both shaking their heads when Yablonski walked in. "Well, what'd you find? Got a damn press conference in an hour. Can't wait all day for you guys to come to me. Crap, looking at the two of you, I'm gonna guess you've got nothing. Am I right? I don't hear anything. Shit, I hate this job." And with that he turned and walked out as quickly as he had entered.

"Wow, that was weird," said Cotter. "The chief didn't yell, and he didn't scream. He simply asked a question, answered it himself, and then walked out. I wonder what's up."

"Yah, sure was something" agreed Partridge. "But enough about the chief. Maybe we need to put this diary down for a minute and check into other angles. Like maybe we need to think about the DNA we found and why it didn't come up with a match."

Cotter scratched his head and looked puzzled. "I thought it didn't come up with a match," he said with some hesitation, "because the person who did this isn't in the data base."

"Did you come up with that on your own?" snickered Partridge.

"No," said Cotter with his annoyance quite noticeable. "The chief came up with it."

"Relax," said Partridge. "What I'm thinking about is maybe, just maybe, our perp was never arrested, so that's why there's nothing in the databank on him, assuming it's a him. Let's chew on that for a while and see where it gets us. We've got nothing to lose. And besides, we're hitting a stone wall on the diary right now anyway."

"Hey," said Cotter, "remember that case down in Truro where they took DNA samples from all the males in town? Maybe we should try that here. If we think the killer could be a first timer, maybe it's someone from the community. What do you think? We might get a hit. And, if certain people refuse, well maybe we can check them out more closely. I mean, at least it's something to move on. Who knows, maybe the chief would give us his blessing."

"We'd need more than his blessings," said Partridge. "I remember that case and all the turmoil it caused. I think it was early in 2004 or 2005, but definitely before I got here. It sure was a mess with some people screaming about their rights and the American Civil Liberties Union getting into the act. And you think the chief will agree to that. I don't think so. God, he'd go crazy with all those people on his back screaming about their rights. You got any other bright ideas?"

When the Weinbergers arrived at the station, it was obvious to both Partridge and Cotter that Mrs. Weinberger was still extremely upset. Partridge ushered them into a private office.

"Thank you for coming so quickly," said Partridge. "We're going to need that letter now. And we need an explanation about why it upset you."

"You tell them," said Judy. "I don't think I can."

"Why don't we just give them the letter," said Phil. "They need it anyway, and then neither of us will have to do any explaining."

Judy nodded in agreement as she reached into her pocket for a tissue.

"This letter from Mary Rafferty to my wife was very personal," said Phil as he handed it to Detective Partridge. "I don't think there's anything in there that will give you a clue about who killed her. But when you read it, I think you'll quickly discover why it upset my wife. Now that you have the letter, we'd like to leave if that's okay with you. Oh, and one more thing. When will the body be released? I mean is there any timeline for this kind of thing? We want to make plans for the funeral? That poor woman deserves a decent burial."

Cotter answered. "As soon as the autopsy is complete and we've gathered all the evidence from the body, it'll be released. The medical examiner is the one who actually releases the body. We'll contact you as soon as we know anything."

"The two of you can certainly leave now," said Partridge. "If we have any questions about the letter, we'll let you know. And thank you for coming over so quickly."

Judy held on to Phil's hand as they left the station and kept repeating the same thing over and over. "Why didn't she tell me? Phil, why didn't she tell me who she was?"

CHAPTER 19

She began to question him a few minutes into their trip to Boston. "Well?"

"Well what?" he said.

"What do you mean well what? The diaries. Clearly I'm talking about the diaries. Did you find the information you needed in her diaries? If you didn't find it, and someone else does, you know we're both screwed."

"No, I didn't find it," he said obviously irritated by her tone.

"You told me it would be easy, remember? Well I guess you were wrong," and she screamed at him. "Now you have three crimes hanging over your head—the original crime that began this whole mess, the bitch's death, and your robbery at the neighbor's house. We're screwed! If they find us, we'll both go to prison. I don't know why the hell I let you talk me into this. Now you've put us both in danger with your crazy idea!"

"Are you finished screaming? People in the other cars can probably hear you, so just cool it. I know what I'm doing, and we won't get caught. There's nothing to tie me to any of the crimes. I'll find what I'm looking for. I'm positive it's in the diaries. Everyone who knew her in the old days knew she wrote her life down in those diaries. She must have used a code. I'll go through them again more carefully. If there's a code, I'll be able to break it, and then we'll be home free. So relax, enjoy the trip into Boston, and concentrate on lifting your new piece. By the way, where do you plan to wear it? No one ever gets dressed with expensive jewelry anymore. Do you plan to fence it?"

"Haven't thought that far," she said. "Probably, but not here on the Cape. It's too small a community, and it could come right back at me. I'm still waiting on money for the stuff I lifted from the clubhouse. No one here knows how to do anything. Should've sent it out to Boston or New York."

"Tried to tell you that," he snickered. "But you're always too smart for your own good. I told you to keep your nose clean and not take anything from here. If they start nosing around you for those thefts, then who would be responsible for screwing up?"

"Okay, okay," she answered back more calmly. "Let's try to enjoy the day. It looks like almost everything from the storm has been cleaned up around here. Hope we have clear sailing to Boston. Maybe we can even grab a bite in the North End. I haven't had good Italian for a long time."

CHAPTER 20

Partridge thought about Cotter's idea of DNA testing at Northridge. The idea had sounded crazy at first, but the investigation was going nowhere fast, and he wondered if it might be worth a shot. It would need the chief's full approval and probably permission from the courts to make sure they weren't stepping on anyone's civil rights.

"Hey Cotter," Partridge said as they were pouring through the diaries once again, "I've been thinking about that DNA testing you suggested even though I thought you were nuts when you first brought it up."

"Well what do you know," said Cotter. "The big city New York cop thinks lowly me from a small town on the Cape might have a decent idea. Will wonders never cease." And then Cotter began to laugh.

"Enough already. I get it," said Partridge after a few moments of listening to Cotter's laughter. "But don't let this go to your head, and don't forget it's not a done deal until we get the chief's approval. We'll run it by him, and we'll say it was your idea—which it was. If he laughs, we'll back off. I don't want to be the butt of jokes in the department."

"That's a deal," said Cotter grinning from ear to ear. "And won't I laugh if the chief gives us his blessings. You know, we're not country bumpkins here on the Cape."

After some coercion on Cotter's part and a lot of fast-talking, the chief got approval for them to do limited DNA testing. He told them to schedule a meeting at Northridge. They decided to bill the meeting as informational. It would be an opportunity to explain where they were in the investigation, and it would open the door, they hoped, to present the idea of DNA testing.

Because the community was still on edge about Mary Rafferty's murder, they were able to schedule the meeting quickly. It was to be held in the main meeting room where there was plenty of room for interested residents to be seated. Partridge and Cotter arrived only a few minutes early. They had learned the hard way that arriving at community meetings too early meant loads of questions they didn't want to answer until the official start, to say nothing about the annoyance of repeating the same thing over and over.

Max met them as they arrived. "Boy if this isn't like deja-vu. How long ago was it that we met like this about Jerry Smith's murder? Mary Rafferty's murder has brought all those memories and frightening thoughts back to those of us who were here at the time. I hope you can give us more information than you did that night. I remember how angry some folks were. They felt it was a waste of time for them to have even come."

Cotter and Partridge exchanged glances. There was no opportunity for them to respond even if they had wanted to since Max was talking so rapidly.

He continued in animated fashion. "Hey, any further news about those things stolen from our clubhouse? Did the lead from down in Orleans ever turn up anything else? I'm sure probably not, because I know you would have let me know if it had. I mean, I know how busy you are, what with the murder of our Mary Rafferty, so the robbery probably isn't that important right now, but I was hoping maybe you had something to share."

Partridge answered, "Sorry Max, nothing yet. We'll let you know when we can. Where would you like us? Don't want to keep the residents waiting. We know they're anxious to hear what we have to say, and there's no need to introduce us. We can take care of that. Maybe though, if you could get everyone's attention."

"Sure, sure," he said. "I'm not the one in charge here, but if you want me to get things moving, I can do that for you. I'll go over and talk to our president. He'll get them quiet so you can begin. You'd think they never had a chance to see and talk to one another. Bunch of gossips is what I say. Sorry, but wouldn't you assume they'd take their seats and stop talking as soon as they saw you come in? It's rude, just rude."

"Maybe they don't know who we are," said Cotter. "We're not in uniform, so perhaps people don't know who we are."

"Good try," laughed Max. "Glance around, detectives. Do you see anyone else in a suit besides the two of you? They sure as hell know who you are. Some of them just don't know when to shut up. You can both sit over here at the table with the microphone."

An elderly gentleman with a crop of white hair and a bunch of folders in his hand walked over as they sat down. "Hi, I'm Butch— Butch Cannidy, just like Butch Cassidy. I get a whole bunch of grief over my name, but I'm too old to change it. My folks never realized what they were doing to me when they gave me the name Butch. I was born years before the movie made the name famous, so I just laugh it off. At least people remember my name. I'm the new president at Northridge. Nice to meet you. I was legally elected a few months ago. Most people wouldn't want the job, but I'm a former administrator from a small school system in Connecticut, so I've some experience. Besides, the wife's gone so I've plenty of time to deal with what's important, as well as the nonsense. Thanks Max. I can take it from here."

Talking into the mike, he said "Folks, folks, please take a seat. I'm sure the detectives don't have a great deal of time for us, and we sure don't want to waste what time they have chatting amongst ourselves. The format will be as follows. First, the presentation by the detectives, and then your questions. And now, let me turn the mike over to Detective Partridge and Detective Cotter, who will take it from here."

Partridge introduced himself and Cotter, and then he proceeded to explain where they were in the investigation. He assured them that it was very early in their search for the killer, but that all of the department's resources as well as assistance from other departments on the Cape were devoting time to find the murderer of Mary Rafferty. "At this time," he said, "the murder does not appear to be a random act."

A hand shot up as Partridge finished his comment about the murder not being random. "I'd like to take all questions at the end, if that makes sense," said Partridge, while smiling at the resident who suddenly stood up and shouted.

"What about DNA? I thought you guys used DNA to solve murders. We're all worried here, and we . . ."

"Sit down Jerry," yelled Max. "We were all told that the detectives would answer our questions at the end. What didn't you understand?"

Partridge and Cotter looked at one another, and then Cotter whispered something to Partridge. This was followed by a nod from Partridge who smiled and said, "We understand your fears and worries, and we're exploring many leads. Unfortunately this is real life and not a television detective show where we solve crimes in an hour. However, this gentleman brought up a very interesting point, and we might as well discuss it now. DNA, as you may or may not know, doesn't solve everything. We do, however, want to pursue that avenue in this case. The DNA that we were able to recover doesn't match anyone currently in the national data base. So, we've decided to collect DNA samples from the residents here in Northridge to further our investigation and rule out certain possibilities."

A clamor erupted amongst most in the audience with some people jumping to their feet. Partridge tried to restore quiet.

"Folks, please. If you can just settle down, Detective Cotter and I will try to answer all questions. I'm sure you'll feel less concerned once you understand the rules surrounding the gathering of DNA samples. Why don't I take the first question from the gentleman who raised the idea of DNA. It was Jerry, wasn't it? Jerry, your last name please."

Jerry stood. "My name is Jerry McCarthy."

"Mr. McCarthy, your question please," said Detective Partridge

"Thank you for calling on me detective, and yes I did raise the question of DNA before anyone else," and he turned and glared at Max.

"Mr. McCarthy?" repeated Partridge.

"Yes, sorry. Well, is it legal to take our DNA? We didn't do anything. We just live here. Most of us didn't even know poor Mrs. Rafferty."

"Yes, it is legal," said Cotter. "There was much controversy around this very idea back in 2005 when investigators decided to collect DNA samples from Truro residents as part of the Christa Worthington murder investigation. For those of you who weren't here on the Cape at that time, or for those of you who don't remember the case, she was a fashion writer from New York who was found stabbed to death. And, despite criticism from the American Civil Liberties Union, a DNA search was undertaken in Truro."

"Perhaps it would be helpful," said Detective Partridge, "if we gave you a little background information about DNA. The United States probably has the world's largest bank of DNA samples, which number in the millions. I don't remember the exact number, but it's probably between five and eight million samples, and most of those samples are from convicted criminals and people who've been arrested. It's similar to a fingerprint and is used widely in the identification of offenders. Some of you may be surprised to know that a single hair is all that is necessary to extract DNA, but we'll be asking for a mouth swab. I'm sure most of you knew all of that anyway, but for some of you who aren't crime readers or fans of detective programs, the information might help clarify what we plan to do here in Northridge. Our sampling will be confined to this community, at first, and specifically to males in this community, but we may need to widen our sample search in the future. Next question," said Partridge.

A woman in the third row stood. "My name is Sue Michaels, and I'd like to know what you'll do with our DNA samples once you're through with them. I mean, we have our personal information stolen whenever there's a credit card security breech and now some of us have to give up our DNA. I'd like to know if anything is private anymore?"

She hit a nerve, and there was a commotion once again.

"Please folks," said Partridge. "We'll respond to all concerns, but you need to give us a little leeway here. We can't have interruptions each time there's a question. To answer Ms Michaels' question, and it was a very good question—any DNA sample, along with all its identifying information like name, sex, and date of birth will be destroyed if we find it doesn't match up to the DNA we found at the crime scene. Next question."

A man next to Sue Michaels asked whether everyone had to submit their DNA. "What if we choose not to give you a sample?" he said.

"Supplying sample DNAs will be voluntary," said Cotter. "There may be a reason for someone to chose not to submit a sample, and we'll certainly keep that in mind during our investigation."

They continued to take questions for another half hour and then explained that they needed to get back to the station. People gathered in small groups as soon as the detectives left. Some grumbled about the DNA sample collections while others seemed comfortable with the explanations they received.

Partridge and Cotter discussed the Northridge meeting as they drove back to the station. "Can't blame those people," said Cotter. "I'd be concerned if I was part of a DNA dragnet. What do you think of the chance that we'll come up with something?"

"You know as well as I do," said Partridge, "the possibility of finding the perp through a dragnet is slim, but we've got to try. The troops over at Northridge are anxious and so is the chief, what with all the media attention on this case. Wouldn't be the least bit surprised, though, if some hot shot with a law background tries to stop us. We'll see what the courts have to say if that happens. Hope we're not stopped. Might get something if we're lucky or if someone panics. That'd be sweet! Meanwhile, what about lunch? I've worked up an appetite. Besides, you did a nice job explaining DNA, so the treats on me. But I pick the place. I love the sandwiches over at Bagel Haven, and the owner is a doll. What do you say?"

"I never say no to a treat," laughed Cotter, "and you know I never say no to food. Like the place myself. We sometimes go there on Sundays after church. They're friendly, tolerant of the mess my little ones make, and they have a great bagel. So you're on."

CHAPTER 21

She and Santiago rode into Boston each deep in his own thoughts following their earlier outbursts. The weather was mild, a typical Indian summer day, and the radio was playing Broadway show tunes. The music reminded her of New York. They had once lived there in an apartment near Lincoln Center. It was small but more than adequate by New York standards. She loved that city with its proximity to theaters, museums, fine restaurants, and Central Park. She had even managed to snatch a Rolex watch from a gullible jeweler there. She wondered if Santiago ever thought of those days. She loved to reminisce, but he had to be in the right mood. It was so annoying. She wished she could just blurt out whatever she was thinking without worrying if the time was right. She decided to take a chance.

"Do you remember the music from *Miss Saigon*?" she said. "Now that was a great play. Remember we sat in the first balcony so we could have a good view of the helicopter on stage. God those seats were expensive, but you agreed they were well worth the price after you stopped grumbling. I wish we were back in the city instead of down here on the Cape. I miss New York."

"You know you're never happy. You're always thinking of wherever you aren't instead of enjoying where you are. My mother was like that. It's why we lived in a million different places, and I never went to the same school for more than two years. What a job I had trying to make friends and figure out who the bullies were. Don't forget, you agreed to come with me to the Cape. So stop complaining. I have enough on my mind trying to find what I need in those damn diaries."

She realized her timing was wrong. He had no desire to reminisce. "Don't worry," she said and patted his knee. "You'll figure everything out; you always do. Hey, why don't we stop and eat now instead of waiting until we get to Boston. I remember we stopped once at a cute little place right off the highway that serves breakfast all day. I don't know the name, but it was on the Easton-Brockton line. You know how much you love breakfast food. What'd you say?"

He agreed. They pulled off the highway and easily found the restaurant. She thought he seemed more upbeat while they were eating, so she kept the conversation casual. When they left the breakfast spot, she glanced across the street. "Isn't that a jewelry store over there?" she said. She was always looking for the right opportunity to snatch a new piece, and it hadn't taken her long on this trip.

"Yah, it's a jeweler, so what?"

"So what? You know what. Pull across to the strip mall and let me check the place out. You know how I love to look."

"Yah, look and touch and take."

"Don't be a grouch," she said. "Just let me see what's there. I promise I won't do anything crazy. You know I'm always careful. If they have to buzz me in, I'll wander around for a few minutes and then walk out. Trust me. You know I'm not stupid."

He pulled the car into the strip mall and parked outside the store. The mall appeared well cared for, even upscale.

He had been to a lot of these places during the years they had been together and had developed a sixth sense. He waited as she got out of the car and went inside. He knew the drill. If she walked out and scratched her head, it meant she had something, and he was supposed to move out slowly so as not to draw attention. If she didn't scratch her head, he could do anything he wanted. They had been through this countless times.

She walked right in. There was no buzzer. A good sign she thought. The jewelry was of high quality in locked display cases. When a salesman approached and asked if he could be of assistance, she smiled and said she was only looking and then casually gave him more information. "It's my big birthday, and my husband said to pick out a trinket. He said he'd come in tomorrow and pay for it. Calls all my pieces trinkets regardless of value. He's so funny. Said to find a piece that made me happy, so here I am. I'm lucky that way." Then she proceeded to meander from case to case. She stopped at one and stared into it for a moment before glancing up to see if the salesman was nearby. She caught his attention and called him over so she could check out a bracelet she had just spotted. "May I try this Yurman piece on? I love this designer. I have several of his rings and of course his earings, but I really love this piece." The salesman carefully removed it from the display case and handed it to her. She oohed and aahed suitably while keeping it on her wrist and pointing to another bracelet by another designer. She tried that one on too, examined both, and then took the last bracelet off while keeping on the Yurman. She tried on and rejected several other bracelets always moving toward those cases closest to the entrance. After trying on another one or two, she smiled at the salesman and said, "This is the one. This is the bracelet I like the best." Suddenly she began to cough, seemingly unable to stop. The salesman asked if she would like a drink of water, and she quickly nodded. As he moved to the back of the store to get her water, she went out the entrance, scratching her head the entire time.

He was ready as soon as he saw her. He had parked so his license plate couldn't be read from inside the store, and they drove off before anyone from the store realized what had happened. He stopped at a gas station after a few miles, and she went into the ladies room and took off her disguise. She had worn a blond wig, heavy makeup, and a tight sweater when she left the Cape, in anticipation of such an event. She even changed her shoes and her handbag before returning to the car, where she took off the bracelet and carefully hid it.

"Are you happy now?" he said. "You know some day you're going to give me a heart attack. I'm getting too old for this shit."

"Don't worry," she said and gave him a peck on the cheek. "I rarely get caught, and besides that place had the worst system ever. The camera that should have been pointing at the front door was turned away, and I stayed out of range of the others. All they'll get is a view of my ass, and the salesman's description will be worthless."

"So are you through for the day?" he said.

"I am sweetie. Let's head into Boston and walk around for a while. Then we can go to the North End for a late lunch and relax. I know how much you love good Italian food, and you deserve a treat."

CHAPTER 22

Partridge and Cotter returned to the station after a fast lunch. They reexamined the diary Mary had placed in the safe-deposit box as well as those the thief had missed at the Weinberger home.

"I don't see anything in this one from the safe deposit box," said Partridge. "It just looks like notes about her everyday life and comments about the Scrabble games she played on the computer. There must be something here, but I'll be damned if I know what it is. It's definitely different from the other diaries we've got and definitely different from those Mrs. Weinberger told us about that were stolen. She said the stolen ones had specific information about the Rafferty woman's life of crime and prostitution."

"Why don't I spend more time looking at all the diaries," said Cotter. "Maybe she used a code. I told you, writing and deciphering codes used to be a hobby of mine. Even thought of joining the FBI once as part of their cryptology department. Believe it or not, even with today's technology, all sorts of criminals still encode messages to hide what they're doing."

"You amaze me," said Partridge. "What other hidden

talents do you have?"

"It's not a hidden talent," laughed Cotter. "It was hidden from you because you never listen to me. I told you about it once, but you probably tuned me out. I think you're in your own head half the time. Is it cause you're thinking about Cynthia? The two of you have been been dating for quite a while, and you seem to spend all your free time with her. Are you going to marry her?"

"When and if we're ready, I'll make sure that you're the first person I tell. And from now on I promise to give you my full attention when you tell me all those important things about your life. Now shut up and go check out the diaries."

"I hear you," said Cotter. "And by the way, a good cryptologist is someone who not only likes to solve puzzles but who also is determined and tenacious. And I am both."

"Stop while you're ahead, hotshot," laughed Partridge. "Really, what are you looking for?"

"Looking for letters, numbers, symbols or maybe even invisible ink that might be hiding a message."

"Interesting," said Partridge. "You know when I was little and took long rides with my parents, they'd give me a special pen and a book with hidden messages. When I rubbed the pen over a page, words would appear. Do you want me to get you one of those pens?"

"Very funny," laughed Cotter. "Actually, some methods include the rearrangement and replacement of words or even the substitution of letters in an attempt to look for and break a code. I'll see what I can find, so don't bother me while I'm working."

"Working?" said Partridge. "That's something new."

CHAPTER 23

Judy was still in shock, but Phil kept her grounded as they planned for Mary's funeral. The medical examiner had released the body to a local funeral home, and Judy, with Phil's help, was making all the arrangements. "I want a small personal funeral for her," said Judy. "She was a private person here at Northridge, so I don't expect many people to attend. I know our friends will come, but let's keep it low key. And nothing religious. She wasn't that kind of person. Does that make sense to you?"

Phil smiled at Judy and gave her a hug. "Go with your gut, and plan whatever feels comfortable. You knew her better than anyone. She's connected to you. You loved her, and we know how much she loved you. I'll support anything you think is best as long as it's within reason."

"I'm almost through writing her obituary, as well as the comments I plan to make at the funeral," said Judy. "I stayed up late working on them. I'll read them to you when I finish. There are facts about Mary that are no one's business, like her years as a prostitute and call girl. She wanted to be who she was here at Northridge, and I'm going to respect that. I can't help what the newspaper might write about her, but I'm going to honor her memory. After the funeral, I want to invite everyone back to our house. It's more personal than a restaurant or renting the clubhouse.

And I want the funeral to be held first thing in the morning. That way we can order brunch platters from Panera Bread, and I can make a noodle pudding. Mary loved my mother's noodle pudding recipe. She always said it reminded her of her mother. I think that would be fitting, don't you?"

"I told you I'd support anything you decided as long as it was within reason. She was important to you, so it's your decision not mine. Tell me what you want me to do."

Judy gave Phil a hug. "I know what you thought about Mary, and I guess we were both right about her. She was a woman with a hidden past. I only wish I'd known who she was while she was alive. I'll always wonder why she kept that part of her life a secret from me. We were so close."

"Don't torture yourself trying to figure it out because you'll never know. What we need to do now is make arrangements for her funeral and burial. The detectives said her body was released to Coastal Funeral. Get dressed, and I'll call to see if we can go over there now. You can finish your writing later. By the way, I think the funeral home writes the obituary for the newspapers, so just concentrate on your comments for the service."

The funeral was held a few days later. Judy was composed as she stood in front of her friends and family as well as Mary's few friends. She began her tribute ...

"Everyone here knows how much Mary meant to me. We only met on the Cape a few years ago, but in that short time I felt a strong connection to her. She was like a mother to me, and she always said she shared those feelings. We spent countless hours in her home as well as mine. We laughed together, played Scrabble together, watched TV together, and went shopping together. Mary and I spoke several times a day, and Phil and I welcomed her into our family. She was with us during holidays as well as most family gatherings. Now she's gone, and I'm devastated. You see, I just learned

something about my dearest Mary that I never knew. It was in a letter she wrote to me that was just found in her safe-deposit box. I learned from the letter that we were related. I learned from the letter that she was my aunt."

There was an audible gasp as Judy relayed the shocking news, and then she broke down and began to cry. Phil rushed to her side and softly asked if she wanted him to finish reading the tribute.

She shook her head, attempting to compose herself and began again. Her voice cracked a few times, but she continued on.

"I wish I had known of our relationship while she was alive, but I guess we both felt it in our hearts. I'll never know why she kept it a secret, and that will always be a mystery for me. What little I do know, I learned from my own mother as I was growing up. I know that Mary was my mother's younger sister and that she left home when she was very young. I remember my mother telling me that the family searched for her for years but never found her. When my grandparents died, as well as other relatives throughout the years, Mary never appeared. My own parents died a few years ago, and there was never any discussion of the lost sister.

She disappeared too many years ago to worry about it now, was always my mother's response. My family was always kind of passive, and my mother said if her sister had wanted to find her family all those years it would not have been difficult. The family had not run away. She could have found them according to my mother. You see, my mother was always angry about the heartache her sister Mary had brought to her parents.

Along with the letter Mary wrote telling me she was my aunt, she also left many diaries describing her life. I learned that she changed her name after she ran away. Her real name was Mary Datonia, and she led quite an interesting life. She gave me the diaries months before she died and asked me not to open them until her death. Phil and I thought this was a little unusual, but we respected her wish. The diaries were buried away in our cellar, and we had forgotten all about them until that awful day.

Mary, rest in peace. We will find out who did this awful thing to you and why. I never loved you as my aunt, but I loved you as a dear friend and you were like a second mother to me. Go with God. "

Mary broke down crying as soon as she finished reading the tribute, and Phil rushed to her side and walked her back to her seat. After the short service, everyone left for the cemetery.

The buzzing amongst Judy's friends and the folks from Northridge who attended the service was more than a whisper, and the general consensus was one of disbelief.

"Oh my God! Poor Judy," whispered Shirley. "She was so good to that woman. I bet that was why Mary moved to Northridge. She probably wanted to be near a relative. I can't begin to imagine how Judy must feel."

"Do you think they looked anything alike?" said Maureen. "I mean, they were close relations. Do you think Judy should have suspected they were related?"

"Are you crazy?" snickered Shirley. "Really, do you look like your mother's sister? You better be careful what you say to Judy when we're at the cemetery and when we're back at her house. She's been through enough without answering dumb questions."

"I guess you woke up on the wrong side of the bed,"

Maureen said. "There was absolutely no need to jump down my throat and make a comment like that. It was a simple question that anyone could have asked, so cool it. I'm going over to talk to Elsie, Mary's friend from cribbage. I don't want to talk to you for a while."

Elsie had been talking to several members of her cribbage group, and she glanced up when she saw Maureen heading her way. She only knew Maureen by sight but knew she was Judy's friend.

"Hi Elsie," said Maureen while smiling and reaching out to shake her hand. "I don't think we've ever met, but I've seen you around and know you were a friend of poor Mary. You're rather new at Northridge aren't you?"

"I am," said Elsie. "I moved in a few months ago and really love living here. People are so friendly, and they welcome newcomers, which not all places seem very good at doing."

"Well I'm glad to hear we're doing a good job. Awful about Mary, isn't it. She was such a sweet person, and Judy was so good to her. Can you believe she was Judy's aunt? The world is full of surprises. I hope they hurry and find out who did this awful thing. Judy is sure going to miss her."

"Mary was very kind to me when I first joined the cribbage group," said Elsie. "She gave me lots of pointers and helped me learn the game. I used to pick her up and take her to the clubhouse for cribbage night. She didn't drive, but I'm sure you knew that. We got to know one another a bit, and she even invited me in a couple times after cribbage. She once told me that her neighbor Judy was the one who made living in Northridge special for her. I guess they had a very close relationship. Mary once told me that she didn't have any relatives, so she probably left all of her jewelry and other valuables to Judy. Hope they find her killer real soon."

"Are you going back to the house after the cemetery?" Maureen said. "Judy invited everyone."

"I don't think so," said Elsie. "I knew Mary, and I wanted to pay my respects, but I didn't know Judy."

"That doesn't matter," said Maureen. "She invited everyone."

"I know, but even if I wanted to, I've got to get to my doctor's appointment in Boston. Thanks for stopping to talk to me and nice meeting you. Maybe we'll connect again. Do you play cribbage?"

"I don't," laughed Maureen. "I'm lousy at games," and she smiled and walked away to search for Judy

CHAPTER 24

There was a mob scene at the Weinberger house after the cemetery, and Judy and Phil were both glad when the day ended.

"Are you okay?" said Phil. "You look like hell. Why don't you lie down, and I'll clean up the mess."

"Thanks, I think I will. I can't believe how exhausting today was. Do you feel the same? I think I'll take the newspaper into the bedroom and glance through it first before I try to nap. Maybe it will help me relax. I feel kind of shaky." With that, she grabbed the paper and left the room.

Phil looked around, not sure where to begin. Although they used paper plates, and Judy's friends had done more than their share to help with the cleaning, there was still a mess. Phil was deep in his own thoughts when Judy came out of the bedroom with the newspaper in hand.

"That was fast," said Phil. "I thought you were going to read a little and then try to nap."

"I was, but check this out in today's *Cape Cod Times*. Someone must have read part of today's paper because it was open to the editorial page when I grabbed it. The headline caught my eye." And she held it up for Phil to see.

DNA Sweep at Northridge in Marshland

The police have a legal right to ask for DNA samples from male residents at the fifty-five plus gated community called Northridge in Marshland, but all citizens there should realize they have the legal right to refuse to comply.

The murder of Mary Rafferty two weeks ago was an awful crime, and it is understandable that the community is frightened. With this fear has obviously come great pressure on the police to solve the murder as quickly as possible.

However justified the need for a quick response, the rights of innocent individuals living in Northridge must be protected. For the police to request such a search so early in this investigation leaves the community vulnerable to abuse if residents do not understand their rights. It also places an additional level of fear on those in the community who wish to exercise their right of refusal, but who worry about casting suspicion on themselves.

The question being raised at this time in the investigation is as follows—have the police exhausted all avenues of investigation prior to requesting DNA from male residents? We certainly hope the answer is yes. All eyes will be on the Marshland Police Force, including those of the American Civil Liberties Union, to make sure there is no coercion in attaining DNA samples.

"Wow!" said Phil. "This is getting political. You'd think they'd give the police a chance to do their work without jumping down their backs. Actually, I'm not sure how I feel about turning over my DNA. But I didn't go to the meeting, so I don't know what my rights are."

"Why wouldn't you turn it over?" said Judy. "You aren't guilty. You didn't do anything, so why do you care?"

"I guess that's what the editorial was about. Reading the paper certainly didn't help you relax did it. Go take a couple of Tylenol and lie down. And remember to unplug the phone so no one disturbs you."

"Okay," she said, "but don't let me sleep too long."

Judy and Phil weren't the only ones who saw the editorial in the local paper. When Partridge and Cotter returned to the station after the funeral, they were met by a storming mad police chief.

"You'd think they'd let us do our work around here. Since the editorial came out, my phone's been ringing off the hook. I've heard from papers all over the damn place as well as the Associated Press and CNN. They want to know why we're requesting DNA samples so early in the investigation. They're asking about the effectiveness of sweeps like the one we're conducting, while citing the high cost of doing what we're doing. CNN also told me, as if I didn't know, that most state labs are already overburdened and understaffed. Does that mean they think we should stop bringing cases to the lab? Christ! I've even been questioned about the Crista Worthington case. Jesus, I hate my job. Now get the hell out of here and solve the damn thing. I gave you what you wanted, so you better not ask me for anything else. And shut the door on your way out!"

CHAPTER 25

They were on their way home from Boston when Alma decided to ask him about the diaries.

"Are you going to yap about them every God-damned minute we're together?" he said. "I'm getting real tired of you and your constant nagging, so just shut up. I don't tell you how to lift your jewelry, so don't you tell me how to do my job. I'll find what I'm looking for. I know what I'm doing, and I know her. She always wrote everything down in those damn diaries. It's in there somewhere."

"Keep your eyes on the road!" she screamed. "You're so busy yelling at me and putting me down that you almost got us both killed. You didn't even see that truck!"

He jerked the car onto the breakdown lane, shut the motor, and grabbed her by the hair. It hurt like hell, and he had a large clump in his hand when he let go.

"I've had it," he said. "One more word out of your mouth, and you'll end up where the bitch ended up, and you've been around me long enough to know I'm capable of doing what I say. I'm sick of your know it all attitude. I drove you around all day like a jerk because you wanted another piece of jewelry. Well let me remind you of a couple things. I'm in charge here, not you. And I call the shots, not you. If you don't like the rules, then leave. But listen to me and listen carefully—if I hear you tell me what to do one more time, we're finished. I don't need you anymore. I've got the diaries, and I'll find what I need. In fact, I might get rid of you right now and save myself the trouble later on. You've served your purpose, and you're getting on my nerves."

She knew she'd pushed him too far. She'd seen it a million times before. He'd be sweet and lovable, she'd say something to annoy him, and he'd go into a rage. She had thought about leaving him for years. But now, now she was really scared. He was blowing more often, and his anger was always directed at her. She knew this most recent rage was because he still hadn't found what he needed in the diaries.

She had thought he was crazy when he first told her about finding Sheila, now known as Mary, after so many years. She remembered the conversation and her shock. "Scrabble? You found her on a Scrabble site? Are you out of your mind? How long are you going to let what you think she knows continue to tear you apart? My God! How old are you now, and how many years ago did all of that happen? She's an old lady, old like you. If she didn't blow the whistle on you before, what makes you think she's still a threat? Forget about her and this crazy Scrabble idea."

"Don't tell me what to do," he had screamed, "and don't lecture me. I need those diaries, and I'll find her myself if you won't help."

She had continued to watch him work the Scrabble site and its chat rooms. And the woman had continued to share her personal information. She had even told him about Northridge when he said he might move to the Cape to be near his daughter. When he discovered her exact location, he became energized.

He knew he needed a woman to work out his plan, so he had lied to Alma. "Do you remember when you came to Vegas to visit me and your diamond watch was stolen?"

"You mean the one I lifted from Mayer's Jewelers in Miami?" she had said. "You know I never found another one like it, and I've looked for years. What I wouldn't give to have that back. It'd bring in a good price today."

"Don't remember where you got it, but boy did you create a scene. You swore that I'd taken the damn thing and nearly got me arrested for it. Never told you cause I couldn't prove it, but always suspected she took the watch. So now, years later, you've got your chance to get even and maybe get it back. Even if she got rid of the damn thing, revenge is sweet. And maybe she'll have some good stuff you can lift."

"I doubt it," she had said. "The woman's old, so she probably has nothing I want. And besides, you don't even know if she's the one who took the watch. Sounds like a whole bunch of baloney to get me to join you. But maybe I can be convinced if you give me a cut of the money you keep talking about."

Giving her a cut was an easy fix for Santiago. If there was incriminating stuff in the diaries, he knew he would get a fortune in blackmail money. And so his plan had been hatched. As for the watch, he had in fact stolen and then pawned it when he was short on cash. Lucky for him, she never learned the truth. They had flown to Boston, driven to the Cape, and she had moved into a rental at Northridge. He stayed totally out of site afraid that this Mary might recognize him even after all these years.

He had explained his plan to Alma—confront this Mary, grab her diaries, and get out. Alma's role was to befriend Mary and acquire any information that would help them get in and out quickly. He knew timing would be everything, so he waited for the right moment. When Alma learned Mary, like many residents at Northridge, never locked her front door, he had the information he needed. Hurricane Sandy was his lucky break.

After the incident in the car when Santiago violently pulled her hair, Alma decided it was time to do something. A double-cross felt like the right something. No one knew of her connection to him; she was simply one of the many widowed residents at Northridge. There would be no way to tie her to Mary's death. He never picked her up at Northridge, and they had rented the unit and her car with an alias. He was blowing at her more often, and she knew someday she could be his next victim. The police were looking for the person who killed Mary, so she decided to lead them to him. She would buy a throw-away phone, call the police, and be scot free. The plan seemed foolproof. She knew the thought of prison was abhorrent to him, so she was sure he would be killed in a shootout. The more she thought about her plan, the more she liked it, and the more she felt it would work. She decided to put it into motion.

She bought the throw away, called the tip in to the police, and sat back to wait. It had all been pretty easy, and she tried not to think about their years together. She was a survivor and life with him had not been that great lately.

CHAPTER 26

The call came into the station late at night. The dispatcher said the voice was muffled, but it sounded like a woman on the phone. The call was short and direct. "You can find the person who killed Mary Rafferty at the Willowbend Motel in Orleans, Unit 15. Be careful. He's armed and would rather die than be captured. And he'd love to take some cops down with him."

The dispatcher was unable to trace the call, and the playbacks revealed nothing more. He immediately called the chief at home.

"This better be good," the chief yelled into the phone. "I finally fall asleep after tossing around half the damn night, and now you. What?"

Yablonski said he'd be right in and directed the dispatcher to call both Partridge and Cotter at home. "Tell them they better get the hell in here," he had barked. Within fifteen minutes they were all in the chief's office discussing their next steps.

Partridge and Cotter both agreed it was a call they couldn't ignore and alerted the Orleans Police. A watch was immediately put on the motel until Partridge and Cotter could get there with backup. Alma had been right. He wouldn't be captured. He was shot trying to escape while firing on the police. A volley of bullets took him down in seconds. A search of the motel room and the car, both registered to a Jack Wiggins, uncovered the stolen diaries written by Mary Rafferty and stolen from the Weinberger residence, as well as several items known to be missing from the Northridge clubhouse.

"Who the hell was this guy and who set him up?" said Yablonski. "Someone out there knows, so you better find him. And call off the DNA sweep over at Northridge. If this guy's DNA isn't a match, we can always reinstitute it. That's one headache off my back for now and hopefully for good. That damn goody two-shoes editor . . . all people like him worry about is not stepping on people's rights. How do they think we solve crimes? It's about time I got out of this business. Too many do-gooders out there interfering with my police work."

Partridge and Cotter spent the better part of the day poring over the diaries found at the motel. Judy Weinberger had remembered some information, but they hoped the actual diaries would shed light on why Mary was targeted and by whom. "Boy," said Cotter, "she was quite a woman. What a shock it must have been for Mrs. Weinberger to read about Mrs. Rafferty's life and then learn that this woman she had come to love as a mother substitute was really her long lost aunt. Quite a skeleton in that closet, I'd say. Wonder which one of these charmers killed her, or if it even was one of them."

"We'll make a list of all the names mentioned," said Partridge. "Then we can divvy up the list and go from there. Someone will have to know something."

"Yah, if we can find them and if they're still alive. Rafferty wasn't young. No guarantee we can find any of these people," said Cotter.

"Thanks for the encouragement," snarled Partridge. "If I began all my New York investigations with your pessimistic attitude, I'd have been thrown off the force in a minute. Now can we get on with the investigation," and he glared at Cotter before going back to the diaries. They had split the pile in half and planned to read one another's piles as a second reading to make sure they didn't miss anything.

The list of possible suspects wasn't very long. Partridge said, "I think we should try and track down this Joey Dee as well as this guy Frank from Miami who she helped put away. They both had a good reason to kill her. And maybe this Smitty lead. Sounds like she was afraid of the people who murdered him. And let's also try and uncover something around the name Sheila Nichols. Maybe we can dig something up around that name. Guess we know what we'll be doing this weekend. And as crazy as it seems, let's investigate this Scrabble connection too."

"What are you thinking?" said Cotter. "You think there could be something there? I've tried to find a code hidden in her last entries where she keeps mentioning Scrabble, but I'll be damned if I can find a thing."

"No, I mentioned Scrabble to continue to entertain you. You know, Cotter, sometimes I don't know how you ever got into this work. It's not only the obvious that we track down. We track down the impossible, and sometimes we find something. You should try it," and he laughed. "Now let's get to work."

"Very funny," said Cotter. "You know sometimes I take revenge on people who amuse themselves at my expense. If I were you, I'd be careful," and he grinned and slapped Partridge on the back. "I'm going to get a cup of that sludge they call coffee around here. Do you want some? And don't worry, I won't poison yours. I plan to be more subtle." And they both laughed.

The next morning they reported their findings to Yablonski. Beyond a short list of suspects derived from Mary Rafferty's writings, the name Sheila Nichols, and a crazy idea about the game of Scrabble—they had nothing definitive. Mary Rafferty's last diary entries had been ramblings about her daily life, suggesting that she was unaware of any imminent danger. There was no clue as to why she had placed a diary into her safe-deposit box, and they suspected that they might never know. Joey Dee, according to Vegas police, had been out of prison for years and had not reported for his last few probation checks. Vegas said they had no idea of his whereabouts. The guy called Frank in the diaries had proven more difficult to track down. Partridge and Cotter were waiting for Miami to fax documents that could lead to his identification. As for Sheila Nichols, they were trying to contact people who might have known Mary under that name. Both detectives had worked through the night to run down leads.

"Did we take Mary Rafferty's computer into custody?" said Cotter after the meeting with Yablonski. "I have an idea."

"Right, of course we did. What's your idea?"

"Well, I was thinking if we can get into it and check out her Scrabble web sites, maybe we can discover something. Those games sometimes have chat rooms. Maybe she was chatting with her killer, and that was how he found her."

"Go for it," said Partridge. "and let me know if you find anything. I'll keep working these other angles. Shit. We've got the guy, but we don't know his connection to the Rafferty woman or why he targeted her. We also don't know who called in that tip and how she was connected to all of this."

CHAPTER 27

Alma heard the news on television as she was getting her breakfast. She had been unable to sleep all night, wondering if he escaped and worried that he was on his way to find her because he realized she was the one who tipped off the police. She wasn't religious, but she prayed all night—"Please get him. Don't let him get away." And then she would have rolling waves of guilt and wonder if she had done the right thing or if she should have kept quiet and just let things happen. But now she knew she had done the right thing. She no longer had to worry about him, and the police would not come looking for her. She had been careful.

She would leave soon, very soon. She would get what was rightfully hers and be gone. A simple robbery. She knew she could pull it off.

Judy stood at the mirror, fixed her hair, and put on her makeup. The routine seemed longer and longer each day, but she never seemed able to speed up the process. And then there was choosing what to wear. Her bed would be littered with clothes as she discarded outfit after outfit searching for the perfect one for the day. She had heard of obsessive compulsive people who went over and over every step in their lives, never satisfied with the results. She often thought that she was becoming one of those people. Phil would get really annoyed. "You're only going food shopping," he liked to say. "Why are you spending so much time fussing?" And then he would give up on her and disappear into his man cave while she got dressed. She was in the middle of her usual self-torture when the phone rang. Phil never answered if she was home. Half dressed and in a quandary over which pair of shoes to wear, she reached for the phone. It was Maureen.

"Did you see it? Did you hear the news?" Maureen was really excited and Judy could barely understand her.

"I don't know what you're talking about," Judy said. "I'm getting dressed, and Phil's waiting for me. I can't talk now. I'll call you later."

"Forget that," Maureen yelled to keep Judy from hanging up. "You have to listen now! They found the killer; the one who murdered Mary. It was down in Orleans. There was a shootout, and he was killed. Someone tipped them off, and the guy ... the killer, shot at the police when they confronted him. One cop was hurt and taken to Cape Cod Hospital. He's going to be okay, they said, but the guy, the killer, he was shot dead. Can you believe all this? It's probably going to be on the next newscast. Do you think the police will call and tell you all about it? You know, because Mary was your aunt."

"Oh my God! When? That bastard! Do they know why he killed Mary?"

"There weren't many details" said Maureen. "They'll probably update with more in the next newscast. I'd try Twitter. They always have information coming on minute by minute."

"What TV station were you watching?" said Judy barely able to contain her excitement. "I have to tell Phil."

"Channel 5," said Maureen, trying to catch her breath. "Call me back if the police contact you. I want to know everything. I mean it, everything."

"Thanks Maureen. I'll talk to you later."

"Phil," Judy yelled, as she ran to find him. "They found the guy. Can you believe it? They found him."

"Slow down. What are you talking about? What guy?"

"The guy who killed Mary—the guy who killed my aunt. That was Maureen on the phone. She heard it on the news. Thank God they got him. And they killed him, Phil. Do you think we'll ever find out who he was and why he murdered Mary?"

"Of course," said Phil. "The police have all kinds of resources to track information like that. They probably won't know for a while, but eventually they'll discover the who and the why. Now promise me Judy, I mean it, no more involvements. We've been through enough, what with Jerry and his murder and now this with Mary. Stick with people we've known for a long time. No new friends with hidden pasts."

"Right, every new person I meet is going to turn out to have a hidden past that ends in murder. You know, sometimes I wonder about you. This was a coincidence. It could have happened to anyone. Are you going to make the same promise to me? Maybe one of the new members at your club has a hidden past. And what about all those guys who come to the house to see your collections, who you hardly know, or the ones who come to buy stuff you put out on eBay? Are you going to put an end to all of that? Right, no answer, so don't lecture. I'm going to turn on Channel 5 and see if there's any further update, and I'm going to call Detectives Partridge and Cotter. I'm a family member, and I have a right to know what's going on."

"Judy, leave them alone. They'll call you if they think they have anything to share. Don't be a pest. You've done enough damage already."

"Stop telling me what to do. I can't stand it when you act like my boss. I can call them if I want to whether or not you think I should."

"Are you coming with me?" Phil said. "Remember, you were getting dressed to go out for breakfast, although it's now taken you so long it's almost time for lunch."

"I'm about ready," she answered back, "but I want to check the TV. If you can't wait, go without me."

"Just make it fast. Go to the local FOX station or that New England channel. They both do breaking news all the time. That's probably better than watching Channel 5. How much more time do you need?"

"I'll be as fast as I can," she said. "There goes the phone. It's probably Shirley. Tell her we know, and I'll call her later. If it's the detectives, I want to talk to them."

"Yah, right," Phil commented snidely. "I'm sure it's probably one of the detectives," but Judy was out of ear shot for the remark.

CHAPTER 28

Alma sat down to contemplate her next move. She thought about all the could haves and might haves as well as how the whole mess had begun. He had told her he was sure that this woman he found on a Scrabble site, and who called herself Mary Rafferty, was the woman he had been looking for all those years. She tried to dissuade him, but he was always stubborn. When something got into his head, he stood his ground.

He had said, "I'm sorry I never told you the truth before today, but I always thought she was the one responsible for stealing your jewelry years ago during one of your visits to Vegas. I couldn't prove it, so I told you to just deal with the loss. Well here's your chance to get even and maybe get some of your jewelry back. I want you to help me."

Alma agreed to join him. If he was wrong about this woman's identity, he said at the very least it would be a great vacation for the two of them.

They bought used low-profile cars in Boston, and each of them secured a second license plate through his connections in case a sudden getaway was needed. He moved to a motel in Orleans under the name of Jack Wiggins, and Alma moved to Northridge also under an assumed name. She had been lucky to locate a furnished rental there. When they needed to get together, they would meet somewhere off Cape. He said those arrangements would be essential if circumstances ever worked against them. Now he was dead, and she prayed there was nothing at the Orleans motel to tie them together. There was no longer a chance for reward money, if there ever was a chance, but at least she no longer had to hear about those ridiculous diaries and what had or had not been written in them.

She was sure the police would have given Mary's personal belongings to Judy Weinberger, so she planned to break into the Weinberger home and hopefully find some of the jewelry that was rightfully hers. She began daily walks past the Weinberger home as well as drive-bys to see if there was a pattern to their movements in and out of the house. She knew they had two cars—the Toyota that was always in the garage and the Honda that was always parked in the driveway. They got into the Honda together most mornings, and on several occasions she followed them to Bagel Haven, a favorite breakfast spot in Marshland. If she could time it correctly, she planned to break in, find what she wanted, and get out before they came home. The correct time came one morning, just two weeks later. Alma was just out her front door when the Honda drove past. She couldn't tell who was in the car, but she had always seen two people at this time of the morning, and the Weinbergers, like most people their age, were creatures of habit. She decided to make her move. Her bags were packed, and she planned to get out of Marshland and the Cape within minutes of leaving the Weinberger home.

She felt lucky when she realized she was wearing her baggy pants with the big pockets and hoped her luck would hold out. Their home backed up to the woods, which meant she would have good cover.

Entrance through the home's back door was easy, and

Alma quickly found her way to the master bedroom where her eyes were drawn to a large jewelry box on the dresser. It had several small drawers and stood about nine inches tall. She had seen similar ones in jewelry and department stores and always wondered who bought them. Now she had found someone. Preoccupied by the jewelry box, she never noticed the closed bathroom door at the far end of the room. She turned quickly when she heard a door open followed by a scream. She was looking straight at Judy Weinberger.

"What are you doing in my house? How did you get in here? What's going on?" Judy cried out while trying to catch her breath.

"Shut up bitch," whispered Alma. "I want what's mine, and I want it now. Where's Mary's jewelry? I know the police gave it to you because you were her only relative. She stole that jewelry from me, and I want it back. I'll give you one minute to hand it over before I get ugly." With that she reached around, grabbed Judy's arm, and twisted it behind her back.

"You're hurting me," Judy screamed. "Are you crazy? I don't know what you're talking about? Mary didn't have any jewelry. I would've known if she had. She always admired mine and even told me that she sold all of hers through the years when she needed money. She didn't have anything. I swear. Now let go of me you lunatic and leave before I scream loud enough to bring in the neighbors."

"No one's going to hear you, bitch," and Alma slapped her across the face. "Now listen to me, and listen well. I want what I want. I know you're lying."

"Who are you?" Judy cried. "I thought you were her friend. I swear you're wrong about her jewelry. Now get out of here before I call the police."

"Look at me closely," said Alma. "Do you think I'm stupid enough to let you get to a phone? You weren't supposed to be home. That was my mistake, but I'm not going to make another one. Lover boy thought Mary had damaging information in her diaries, but he couldn't find what he was looking for. I'm not going to run into the same dead end. Now where is it?" And she twisted Judy's arm again.

They were both startled when they heard the front door open and Phil shout, "Judy, I'm back. I forgot my phone. Have you seen it? Are you in the bedroom?"

"What the hell's going on?" he yelled when he saw Judy. "Let go of my wife! Are you crazy?" And he quickly reached under his jacket and pulled out a gun. "You better let go of her, and … and do it now," he said.

Alma instantly let go and tried to explain, hoping to somehow get away, but Phil wasn't buying her explanation. She had walked right into a mess, a mess of her own doing.

"Judy," said Phil anxiously, "call the police and tell them to get right here. Don't waste any time. Just call 911 and hurry."

Partridge and Cotter were at the station when the call came in, and they followed the squad car to Northridge and the Weinberger home where they found Mr. Weinberger holding a woman at gunpoint.

"Mr. Weinberger, put the gun down," said the officer. "We'll take over from here. Now exactly what's going on?"

There was a sudden scuffle as Alma tried to reach for Phil's gun. The officer quickly put her down.

"Okay, how about we all sit down and explain this little scenario before someone gets hurt. Detectives, do you guys want to take over or should I do the questioning?"

"I'll take over. Thanks, Jeff," said Partridge. "Mr. Weinberger, because you were the one with the gun, why don't you begin and tell us how come you're carrying."

"Well, first of all, I was carrying because I have a permit to carry a concealed weapon. I was on my way to

Boston, and I like to carry when I go to the city. You know how it is. I always think, what if I run into something, and I need to protect myself. Besides, it's good practice for the concealed weapon course I'm taking over at Cape Region Gun Club. I'm sure you know the place. A few of your guys on the force belong there."

"Mr. Weinberger," said Detective Cotter, "let's try and stay focused on what happened here. Now if you would, please explain why your gun was pointed at this woman."

"Well, I forgot my phone, and Judy always gets annoyed when I don't have it with me, so I came home to get it. When I opened the door, I found this crazy lady holding my wife in an arm lock. I could see she was hurting Judy, so I pulled out my gun to make her let go."

"Okay, Mr. Weinberger. Now, Mrs. Weinberger, if you would, please tell us what happened before your husband entered the house," said Cotter.

"Thank God Phil got here in time. I don't know what might have happened otherwise," and she leered at Alma. "I was coming out of the bathroom when I saw this . . . this lunatic going through my jewelry. I screamed, and then she grabbed my arm and twisted it behind my back and told me some ridiculous story about Mary's jewelry belonging to her. I don't know anything about jewelry she says my aunt was supposed to have stolen. I don't understand any of this."

Partridge turned toward the intruder. "I'm Detective Partridge ma'am, and your name please?"

"I'm not talking to anyone without a lawyer," Alma stated while crossing her arms and trying to look defiant. "I'm not saying anything. I know my rights."

Judy piped in. "Her name is Elsie, Elsie Francheska, and she lives here at Northridge. She used to pick my aunt up every Wednesday night and drive her to the clubhouse, where they both played cribbage. I thought she was my aunt's friend. I used to drive my aunt Mary to cribbage on my way to art lessons, but then Mary told me about this new resident, Elsie here, who had offered to drive her both ways, so I stopped driving. That's all I know about her. She even came to Mary's funeral."

"Is that correct?" said Partridge. "I hope you realize it's a crime to give a false identity."

"I told you," said Elsie, "I'm not talking without my lawyer."

"Well, whoever you are," said Partridge, "we have to take you into custody for breaking and entering into the Weinberger home and for threatening bodily harm to Mrs. Weinberger here. We'll straighten this whole mess out with you and your lawyer when he or she arrives. Until then, we'll try to make you nice and comfortable at the station. I trust you won't make us wait too long for your lawyer to arrive." Partridge then nodded at the officer, who proceeded to read her rights and handcuffed her before leading her outside and placing her into the cruiser.

"Thank you Mr. and Mrs. Weinberger," smiled Detective Partridge. "And Mr. Weinberger, please be careful with that gun and who you pull it on. There could be problems if you pull it on the wrong person or if that person tries to grab it and turn it on you."

With that last comment, they left the Weinberger home with Elsie Francheska in tow. A small crowd had gathered outside the Weinberger home when word spread that police cars had sped into Northridge and parked in front of their home. The chatter amongst the bystanders focused on Mary Rafferty's murder and her still unidentified killer as well as the robbery at the Weinberger home. This latest incident was giving the community even more to talk about.

All those present outside the Weinberger home gasped when Elsie Francheska was placed into the cruiser. They weren't the only ones. On the ride back to the station Cotter said, "Holy shit, is this case bizarre or what? Maybe this Francheska woman can put it all together for us. I bet if we lean on her a bit we'll discover she was the mystery caller that lead to our guy's demise. Sure would love to clean this one up before it gets any weirder, and I know we don't want to go back to thinking about that DNA sweep. Don't think the chief could live through the publicity or the pressure."

"You're probably right about doing the DNA sweep," said Partridge. "This latest development feels like it might be a real good lead. That woman better hurry up and get her lawyer in here. I'm itching to find out what she knows."

As soon as the police left, Judy fell apart. "Oh my God, when I think of what could have happened if you hadn't come back for your phone. This is getting scarier by the minute. That woman is crazy. I think she could have really hurt me if I didn't give her what she wanted. I didn't know what she was talking about, and the more I said that, the angrier she got. She was always so nice to Mary, taking her to cribbage every week. Mary never said she had known her before. Maybe the woman had Mary mixed up with someone else, or maybe she was stalking Mary. It's unbelievable!"

"You're telling me," he said. "I'm just glad I came back in time. The police have her now, and hopefully they'll find out the real story. Obviously, she's more than this sweet lady Elsie who used to drive Mary to her cribbage game. Are you okay? Did she hurt you? Do you think we should check you out?"

"No, I'm fine," Judy said, "but I want to take a hot shower. I can still feel that crazy woman's hands on me. You aren't going to Boston now, are you? I don't want to be alone."

"Of course not. What do you take me for?" and he

gave her a hug. "The police didn't say anything about needing us, so after your shower, how about we take a ride down Cape and grab lunch somewhere along the water. I think the change of scenery might help. What do you say?"

"Thanks," she said. "You know, sometimes you can be such a nice guy. I guess that's why I still love you," and she went over and gave him a big hug.

The phone rang as she was getting ready for her shower, and she reached for it out of habit. It was Shirley.

"Is it true what I heard?" Shirley said. "Did Elsie break into your house and threaten you? Maureen called me. She was at aerobics when Tina burst in with the story. Maureen said she was on her way to your house to hear all about it. I thought I'd call to warn you in case you didn't want company. You know, so Phil could cut her off at the door. So, is it true?"

"Yup, can you imagine? I think this Elsie woman must be crazy or something. I was terrified. I don't know what would have happened if Phil hadn't come in. Shirley, Phil pulled his gun on her. Can you believe that? He was carrying because he was on his way to Boston. I didn't know he had a gun when he left the house. I hate when he carries. It makes me nervous as hell. He knows how I feel about it, so he never mentions it. But I don't think I'm ever going to complain about it again. I have to go, Shirley. Thanks for telling me about Maureen coming over. Phil will grab her at the door. You caught me as I was going into the shower. I need to wash away the feel of that woman. And then Phil and I are going to take a ride down Cape and go somewhere for lunch. I need to get away for a couple of hours. Phil thought a change of scenery would help me relax. He can be a real sweetheart sometimes. I'll call you tomorrow." And she hung up.

Judy yelled to Phil so he could head Maureen off at the door. "Phil, that was Shirley on the phone. She said

Maureen was on her way over. Please tell her I'll call tomorrow. If she comes in, we'll never get rid of her. You know how she likes to talk. I'm going to take that shower now."

The doorbell rang as soon as Judy turned on the shower. Phil answered and explained to Maureen that Judy would call the next day and that everything she had heard was true. He explained how he had returned home for his phone and come upon Elsie threatening Judy and asking for some jewelry that Mary had supposedly stolen.

"You know, that's funny," said Maureen. "I was talking to Elsie at the funeral, and she said something about Mary probably leaving all her jewelry to Judy because Judy was Mary's only relative. At the time I thought it was a strange thing to say, but then I forgot all about it. Do you think she was planning this for a while? Do you think I should tell the police?"

"Probably a good idea," said Phil. "Ask to talk to Detective Partridge or Cotter. They're the ones working on the case."

With that, Maureen left and Phil yelled to Judy that Maureen was gone. "Hurry up," he said, "before anyone else comes to the door or calls. It's already getting late. If we're going to get lunch down Cape while they're still serving, you better move it."

CHAPTER 29

Partridge and Cotter arrived at the station with the Francheska woman in tow. She had been read her rights and the preliminary search, the 'pat down', had not revealed a concealed weapon. A full-blown search at the station also failed to turn up a weapon. She was booked and charged for breaking and entering as well as threatening bodily harm, while continuing to insist that she would not talk without the presence of her lawyer. Meanwhile, Partridge and Cotter discussed her case with the chief.

"I hope this woman is the break you guys need to bring this case to rest. My ulcer can't take any more harassment from those people over at Northridge. Do they think we're just sitting on our asses waiting for the crime to solve itself? So talk to me. What do you think you've got here in this Francheska woman?"

"We hope to tie her to that anonymous call that resulted in the other night's shootout," said Partridge. "We still don't know who the guy was. We're waiting on fingerprint and DNA analysis to give us something. And if she made the call, we don't know how they knew each other or if she was somehow involved in the Rafferty murder. We'll see if we can connect it all. We're waiting on her lawyer now. Says she won't talk to us without him."

"Was the Weinberger woman hurt or just shaken up?"

inquired the chief. "She sure manages to get herself involved. What kind of unlucky star does she live under?"

"It sure seems that way," laughed Partridge. "She was in pretty rough shape and real lucky that her husband came back when he did. He was like a regular hero to her, what with his gun and all. Lucky for him that it was registered and that he had a permit to carry. Would have hated to take him in with the Francheska woman."

"What about a search warrant for the woman's house. Is that in process?" said the chief.

"Yup," said Cotter. "We're waiting on the judge now."

"Well," the chief said, standing up from his desk, "let me know if you come up with anything else. Hey Partridge, I've been meaning to tell you that my sister's happy as a clam since she's been going out with you. And the whole family appreciates the time you've spent with the kids. She tells us they're doing much better in school this year."

Partridge smiled and said, "and Chief, have you noticed I'm also much happier? We both have lots of fun together, and those kids are great. But I guess I'll be putting tonight's plans on hold if this case breaks in the next few hours."

"Honest, Chief. I can vouch for how much happier he's become," laughed Cotter. "God, sometimes he even respects my opinion."

"Whatever," said the chief. "First solve the case, and then you can go back to entertaining my sister and torturing one another. I've got more important things to do than yack with the two of you all day. Now get out of here."

The call came into Cotter a few minutes after he arrived back at the office he shared with Partridge and two other detectives. It was a fairly good sized office, considering the size of the entire Marshland police station. Each detective had a metal desk, which had probably been around for years, and a chair covered in cheap leather, now cracked and peeling from years of use. File cabinets lined the wall. Cotter picked up his phone. Although the quarters were close, they had all learned to focus on their own conversations and block out those of others.

"Hey Cotter, it's O'Brien. Just finished checking out some of the files on this guy's laptop—the guy from the shoot-out in Orleans. Seems he liked to play Scrabble a lot, just like the Rafferty woman. We got a warrant and contacted the online game people and got a hit. Appears he played the game with her. Probably stalking her. Don't know how that happened, but people today give away all kinds of information while they're online. We're still pulling the hard drive apart and analyzing stuff, but I thought I'd ring you up and fill you in on the Scrabble angle. There was also a chat going on between them as they played. I'll send you the print out from all their games. You know the case, so maybe you can read something into it. I've also got a list of places he Googled and sites he visited. Send you that too. When you put together a cluster graph, it should help you track where he was before arriving in Marshland. I'm faxing it all now."

Cotter filled Partridge in on what he had just learned. Suddenly they had more leads.

"Now wouldn't it be great if the Francheska woman talked," said Cotter sounding more than a little excited. "I'm beginning to feel like this case is breaking our way. Sure would be nice to bring it to the chief real soon. He does get a lot of crap from the locals."

"Feeling sorry for him?" snickered Partridge. "You do realize, I hope, that he gets paid for dealing with aggravation and paid pretty well, last time I checked the town report. So stop feeling sorry for him. Let's go check on our guest and see how she's doing. Maybe we can make nice and get her to say something."

"Ms Francheska, we've got a search warrant for your

house," Partridge said. "So, before we rip the place apart, is there anything you'd like to tell us?"

"Go fuck yourself," she growled. "Are you stupid or something, or do you think I'm stupid. I told you, I don't say nothing without my lawyer. I know my rights. You're not allowed to question me until my lawyer gets here. I know how this works. I know all about your loaded question. You're going to try and get me to say something incriminating. Been there. Done that. You'll have to let me go once my attorney gets here, so get the hell out of here now and stop bothering me!"

"Suit yourself," said Partridge, and they left her.

"Piece of work," said Cotter. "Hope she never brought a kid into this world. Wouldn't like to think of another one like her out there."

Information came in later that day about the guy who had been shot and killed in Orleans, and they shared it with the chief.

"So this is what we know so far," said Partridge. "We ran the prints and discovered that the guy's real name is Jack Santiago, and he's wanted on a warrant for murder. And surprise, surprise—seems his long-time girlfriend is a pretty well known jewelry crook. And get this—she's currently out on probation, and they've been looking for her on failure to report to her probation officer. We're still waiting on this Francheska woman's prints, but we're pretty damn sure she's this Santiago's girlfriend. If so, this will connect all the dots. Now we just need to get her to talk so we can pull all of this together. We're waiting on her lawyer. We think we can probably get her as an accessory on the Rafferty murder, but we need to find out why Rafferty was murdered."

"Good job," said the chief, while trying to clear his throat. "This damn cough of mine. Can't seem to get rid of it. The wife says I smoke too much, but I don't listen. She's like most wives, always telling you what to do. You have that issue Cotter?"

Cotter and Partridge stole a glance at one another, and Cotter answered. "Know what you're saying, Chief. Mine's always telling me to stop eating so much junk. She doesn't understand how much I love the stuff. It makes me happy."

"Okay, you guys, back to the case. I'm thinking there might be some talk of a plea bargain here. Your Francheska dame's got a lot of explaining to do. Maybe she'll spill the beans to save herself."

"Hope so," said Partridge. "The guy killed in Orleans had the Rafferty woman's diaries. You know, the ones stolen from the Weinberger house. Evidently wanted something in them real bad. We've been combing those diaries but haven't found a thing to explain why she was killed or why he took the chance of getting caught by hanging around to steal them. It doesn't add up."

"He might have gotten away with murder if he had stayed clean after the initial crime, but they never do. They think they're smarter than they really are, and most of them get caught due to their own stupidity," said the chief. "You know where to find me if anything develops, so go earn your pay!"

They let Elsie Francheska stew in her cell for the rest of the day and most of the following day.

She only wanted who she referred to as her own personal lawyer. "Don't trust any court appointed lawyer," she had snarled. "I'll just enjoy your fine accommodations until he gets here. We've been around the bend a few times, and I trust him. Don't know the quality of what you've got down here on the Cape," and she emphasized the word Cape with a sarcastic twist to her voice.

Her lawyer finally arrived from somewhere out of state and, after producing his proof to practice in Massachusetts, Cotter and Partridge got down to the business of what the chief referred to as earning their pay.

The lawyer, a James Fitzgerald, was a smooth talker and a smooth dresser—definitely not typical of anyone Cotter was used to working with on the Cape. Partridge, on the other hand, knew the type. He had seen loads of smooth talking lawyers from his New York days, and he thought it might be fun to match wits. He had always been pretty good at it in his previous life. In fact, the guys had often deferred to him because of his reputation for being a hardnose during plea bargaining. Partridge explained that he was the lead detective on the case and that all discussions and any plea bargaining would go through him. He then led the lawyer to where they were holding the Francheska woman and left them alone to become reacquainted. It didn't take the lawyer very long before he signaled for Partridge. It always worked that way—psych out the other side and then negotiate for your client.

Partridge explained the charges against the woman and also asked how long the lawyer had been representing her. "It's not often we wait this long for a lawyer to arrive," Partridge said while trying to exude an image of the small town detective. "You must really be someone special to her. If there's going to be a wait for someone's lawyer, we usually get their permission to have a court appointed lawyer assigned. Have you been her lawyer for a long time?"

"Come now, Detective Partridge. It is Partridge isn't it? You know better than to question me like that. What do you say we cut the crap and cut to the chase. I assume you fellows up here on Cape Cod understand what I mean. So what have you got, and what will it take to get my client on her way out of here and off the Cape. I understand things haven't been that hospitable for her in your jail."

"Well, for starters," smiled Partridge, "how about she comes clean about who she is. We know Elsie Francheska is just a convenient name. So, at the very least, we've got her on false identity charges. Let's follow that up with what she was doing breaking into someone's home. When we have that bit of information, maybe we can talk specifics about our hospitality."

"Fair enough," said Fitzgerald. "I know my client is anxious to return to her winter home. She told me this was her first time on the Cape and probably would never return."

"What a shame," replied Partridge, not trying to hide his sarcasm. "Speaking for myself and my partner, we rather enjoyed spending time with her, but we understand that she probably doesn't agree with our sentiments. Let us know when she's ready to come clean. We have quite a few questions for her. And tell your client there will be no plea bargain unless we get the full story, including her connection to Jack Santiago and the murder of Mary Rafferty. With this guy Santiago dead, we might even charge her as an accessory to the woman's murder. So with that hanging over her head, it's probably a good thing she waited for her own lawyer—a lawyer who knows her so well. We here on the Cape wouldn't want her represented by anyone but the very best."

"If you'll excuse me," smiled Fitzgerald, "I'd like to see my client again."

"Wow," said Cotter, "what a sleaze. Acts like he thinks he's better than attorneys we have on the Cape. I'd put ours against him any day."

"Just business," laughed Partridge. "Seen them all— the good, the bad, and the ugly. He probably is good at what he does. Bet he's got a whole client list of the bad and the really ugly. Just a hunch, but something tells me I'm right."

"*The Good, the Bad and the Ugly* was one of the greatest spaghetti westerns of all times," said Cotter. "Saw it years ago and then caught it again on The Movie Channel. Love the part when Eastwood says, "make my day." They don't make movies like that any more. I miss seeing people like Clint Eastwood. And don't forget John Wayne, a hell of an actor."

"Boy are you dating yourself," teased Partridge. "John Wayne, God I don't remember the last time I heard his name. I used to go to the movies with my dad. He loved those westerns and war movies with John Wayne. My mother hated them, and because dad didn't like to go alone, I was elected to keep him company. I didn't mind, though. It gave me some special time with him, and now I have those memories. But enough of that. Our friendly visiting lawyer and his client should be ready for us soon."

Partridge had no sooner uttered those words when the duty officer announced that Fitzgerald and the suspect were ready to speak to them.

CHAPTER 30

Judy and Phil agreed to join their close friends for an early dinner. Everyone was anxious to hear how Phil had saved Judy. Phil suggested they all go to Siena at the Commons.

"The pizza is good as well as the drinks, and the noise level on a Saturday night should hopefully prevent people from eavesdropping on our conversation. What do you think?"

"What I really want to do," Judy said, "is get out of the house and away from here. I need to stop living this nightmare. I think we should take a trip somewhere."

"Are you serious?" said Phil while practically jumping at her. "You're always looking for a chance to go somewhere. You certainly are a travel slut, and you never disappoint. Where does the lady think she'd like to travel this time?"

"Anywhere, and why are you being so nasty? This has been awful for me, and I need to try and put it behind me. I don't think I can do that while looking at Mary's house everyday and seeing that awful woman Elsie, or whatever her name is, threatening me in our bedroom. So I'm serious about getting away from here for a little while. I'll go anywhere you're willing to go. And if you need some itinerary suggestions, I'd be more than happy to help. We've talked about Calgary and the Lake Louise area more than once. How about that trip? With the world in such a mess, that's a safe low budget trip, although I guess it doesn't make sense for this time of year. I know—how about the islands? We've never been, and it always sounded like a great place to unwind."

"Refresh my memory," interrupted Phil. "Exactly when did we talk about a trip to Calgary and Lake Louise? Seems you've talked about it, not me. And, as for the islands, you know I hate the heat and can't sit on the beach doing nothing for hours. So you can scratch that idea. And besides, why the hell are we talking about a vacation? That's a far cry from deciding where the group should go for dinner. Sorry, but it's annoying the way you always try to manipulate a conversation."

"Excuse me," snapped Judy. "Let's tone this conversation down some. We've both been through quite a bit lately, and it's not over yet. If we keep this up—I'll get mad, slam the bedroom door, and tell you to go to dinner without me. How about we call a truce before this escalates any further?"

"You know you really have no sense of humor," said Phil. "I was just trying to distract you from what happened in our house with that Francheska woman and all the other crap that's gone on since the storm and Mary's murder. I guess it was a bad idea. What do you say we start over. So, what do you think about my idea of Siena for dinner with our friends? If you don't want to order pizza, we can do a salad and calamari. You always say their calamari is the best you've ever had. Or the salad and scallops. That's not fattening. What do you think?"

"Siena is fine, but sometimes you annoy the hell out of

me. You put me down, and when I get annoyed, you tell me that I don't have a sense of humor. It's enough Phil. It's really enough. I'm tired of it, and on top of what I've been through, it's downright mean. If you were more sympathetic, you'd understand that I probably would benefit from a change of scenery. Remember, Mary was like a mother to me. And now that she's gone, and now that I know who she was, you've got to realize that I'm really in mourning. So cool it!"

"Okay, but what about Siena?"

"You always try to appease me and say okay, but you keep on doing it. Say you're sorry and give me a hug. I need a hug."

Before Phil could respond, the phone rang and Judy answered it.

"Hi Shirley . . . right, we were talking about it. Phil suggested Siena. If that's good for everyone, we can all meet about six. Why don't you get the reservation and call us if the time doesn't work."

"I'm still waiting for that hug," Judy said, after she hung up from Shirley. "I really need one, and I think you really need my forgiveness."

After much hugging and a few tears, Judy left to shower and get ready for dinner. She hoped her need to get out of the house for a change of scenery would not be ruined by focusing the entire night on her dramatic rescue, as well as a rehash of Mary's murder.

CHAPTER 31

"My client says she has information for you," said Fitzgerald, "but first she wants assurance that all charges against her will be dropped and she'll be allowed to leave the state."

"Don't know the information your client has," said Partridge, "and you know it's not our decision. But how about giving us a clue about what she knows, and we'll see what we can do."

"My client feels she has knowledge that will shed light on not only the murder of Ms. Rafferty but will also prove of interest to other police departments in the country. What can you do for her if she give that to you?" said Fitzgerald.

Partridge answered. "Elsie, may I call you Elsie?"

"Sure," she sneered, "as long as I can call you by your first name. Otherwise it's Ms. Francheska if you don't mind." And she emphasized 'if you don't mind' with more than a bit of sarcasm.

"Certainly," said Partridge. "Now Ms. Francheska, as we explained to you several times, we don't have the final authority to promise you anything. I'm sure you know only a judge can do that. However, what we can do—if the information is as valuable as you say it is—what we can do is recommend leniency during a plea bargaining session because you helped us out here. If we can all agree on that, then I think we can proceed."

Elsie looked at attorney Fitzgerald. He leaned over and whispered something in her ear, and she answered back with "Yah, yah, I get it. Let's get it over with."

"We'll be electronically recording your statement in its entirety," said Cotter. "We ask that you take your time telling us your side of the story and what you know about other events leading to Ms. Rafferty's death. We'll have a pitcher of water and a glass for you in a few minutes, so feel free to begin whenever you feel comfortable."

"I guess a cocktail is out of the question," and she snickered.

Partridge and Cotter began to salivate as she told a story of murder, prostitution, and robbery.

"I never knew Mary before arriving in Northridge. I was told to become her friend and not to be obvious."

"Who told you to become her friend?" said Cotter.

She glanced at her lawyer, shook her head, and let out a big sigh. "Are you going to stop me every two seconds to ask a question?" Elsie said, sounding annoyed. "You're interrupting my train of thought."

The detectives agreed to hold all questions until the end of her story.

"I'll start again," she said, and continued with her story. "It took a little time and a little questioning, but I found out that Mary liked cribbage. Never heard of the damn game, but I joined the group and learned to play as a way to become her friend. I heard someone say Mary didn't have a car and needed rides, so I offered to pick her up whenever there was a game. In a short time we became cribbage friends, and she told me about her neighbor Judy who had become like family to her. I didn't question her about anything, and she really didn't tell me very much. Actually, she didn't ask me much, either, and I kind of liked that about her. Too many people around here are just plain nosy. You'd be surprised what they want to know. Where did you live before the Cape? How many children do you have? What was your job? Before I knew it they were moving onto things like whether I own stocks, get a pension, or even why I'm not married. You wouldn't believe the nerve of some of these people."

"Ms. Francheska," said Partridge, "I think we can move ahead with this more quickly if you would try to stay focused on the topic."

She gave him a snide look and then continued. "While Mary and I had this kind of neighborly thing going on, my friend was waiting for the right time to break into her house and get those notebook things that some people write in every day. Me—I'm not a writer and never was. Don't understand the need to rehash the day. Over is over, but I guess some people can't let things go. Whatever. When we heard there was a hurricane coming, my friend said the storm would be the perfect time to break in and get what he needed. He said the rain and the wind would cover any noise. I told him that breaking in would be easy because Mary never locked her door. Stupid woman! She came right out and told me. 'Elsie,' she said, 'the hearing's not what it used to be. So, if I don't come right out, I probably didn't hear the horn. Just come in and get me.' I usually had to get her. Got the lay of the land, so to speak, and passed the information along to my friend. Discovering the open door thing was a stroke of luck." She stopped to take a sip of water. "Think I can get some ice? Where'd you get this crap? It's awful. You trying to poison me or something?"

"We'll see what we can do," smiled Partridge. "Detective Cotter, will you see if the ice machine has been fixed," and he cleared his throat as a prearranged signal to Cotter.

"As I was saying, my friend got a lot of information from me. I liked to remind him that without me he'd have been caught while trying to break into her house. Well, he didn't find the stuff he wanted and said he killed her out of anger and frustration. I thought that was pretty stupid, but what was done was done. I told him about Mary's friendship with her neighbor, and we both thought the neighbor's house might be a good place to look. You know, maybe she gave them to the woman for safekeeping. I mean, they were close. Christ, what a shock that was to find out Mary was her long lost aunt. A real tearjerker if I ever heard one. Next thing you know they'll be making a movie about it. Sure is a crazy world."

"Ms. Francheska," Detective Partridge said while raising his eyebrows in a questioning expression.

"Yah, right. Well, he found some of those notebooks in the Weinberger house and managed to get in and out without being caught. He spent hours reading the damn things. Said he needed to find just the right information. Never did find it, and boy was he bull. He told me that years ago his boss had offered a reward to anyone who found Mary and her diaries. That's the word he used, diaries. Couldn't think of it before. Well anyway, his boss, and he never said who the boss was, had promised a bundle of money for the diaries if and only if they contained specific information about the murder of some prostitutes in Vegas. That's why he was so bull. He couldn't find anything that named this boss as responsible. That meant there wouldn't be the bundle of money he had been dreaming of for years. The poor sucker found Mary quite by accident one night while playing Scrabble online. She wasn't known as Mary back then, but he was sure he had the right woman. He talked me into joining him. Said if he was right, he'd be able to share a bundle with me. Said once he found the information he needed, he'd blackmail the guy who originally offered the reward. Said Mary's information would really be worth big bucks now because the guy had became a politician or something."

"We'll be sitting pretty once I get my hands on that stuff," he liked to say. "Just wait. I'll buy you the best jewelry."

"I asked who the politician was and exactly what information he was looking for, but he wouldn't tell me. Said it was too dangerous for me to know. Then one day he casually mentioned the name Mitchell. Don't know who this Mitchell is, but that's not my problem now. Well anyway, he said Mitchell would be shocked that Mary and the diaries had been found after so many years. When he found nothing incriminating in them involving this guy Mitchell, he became a crazy man. He threatened me and said I had served my purpose. I was afraid of what he might do to me and afraid that he might name me as an accomplice in the murder and the robbery if he got picked up. So I called you and left an anonymous message about where to find him. I knew there would be a shootout, and I knew he wouldn't let himself be taken. Although we've been together for a long time, taking care of myself has always been my first priority. I wouldn't be sitting here now if I left right after my phone call. Pretty stupid of me, I guess. But I always loved jewelry, and he said she was the one who stole mine years ago in Vegas. I only wanted back what was mine.

"That's all I'm gonna say. You find this Mitchell politician, and I bet you open up a real can of worms. Might even get yourselves promoted. So what do you say? Have I broken this case out for you?"

"Time will tell," said Partridge. "Time will tell. But for now, we have to charge you with accessory to murder as well as breaking and entering with intent to commit bodily harm. Your arraignment will be held within 48 hours, and until then I guess you're our guest."

"You bastards! You lied!" she screamed as she was lead away.

Partridge and Cotter connected with the chief following the interview and filled him in.

"Well," Yablonski said, "did she know anything? Was she helpful?"

"For sure, for sure," laughed Cotter.

"Well, is it a secret? Are you going to tell me?"

Partridge said, "I'll start Cotter, and you fill in with anything I leave out."

"We got some good information, Chief. The woman knew more than we gave her credit for when she was first arrested at the Weinberger home," and he filled him in on all aspects of her testimony, including the bombshell about the politician. "Cotter and I will try to locate this Mitchell guy and see if we can connect him to Santiago, the guy we took down in Orleans."

"Good work, good work," said Yablonski. "Keep me in the loop," and he shooed them out of his office.

A brief search brought up several politicians with either a first or last name of Mitchell. Partridge and Cotter split the list and made phone calls to police and newspapers in the listed cities and towns.

"Hope this doesn't take too long," laughed Cotter. "My daughter has a soccer game today. Promised the wife I'd be there and promised Emily. She doesn't always understand why I can't be at all her games. She says she understands the work I do, but then in typical eight year old fashion makes me feel like a crummy father for not showing up."

"Sounds like she's got you wrapped around her finger," said Partridge. "Maybe you need to do a better job explaining your job."

"When did you become an expert on raising a daughter?" laughed Cotter. "Cripes, you never had kids, and from what you said, you were a lousy husband who always let his police work overshadow his marriage."

"Cheap shot, Cotter. But now I'm a changed man. I always call Cynthia if I have to break a date and always make it up to her. I've even managed to go to a fair amount of her kid's games. So I do know a thing or two about managing family dynamics with my police work. Better do a better job explaining to your kid because we're not going anywhere until we locate this Mitchell guy."

"Really boss?" said Cotter.

"Really son," said Partridge.

And they both laughed.

Cotter felt he had one very good lead while the rest of the names looked like dead ends. His one possible lead was a guy from a small town in central Utah running for a local seat on the board of selectman. His name was Stephen Mitchell. According to the local paper, he was the incumbent and everyone expected him to win. The editor at the St. Claville Times told him that Mitchell owned a local restaurant in town and was quite popular. Clean sheet, according to the editor, except for accusations of cruelty and abuse from his former wife.

Partridge, on another telephone line, came up with two leads. His first guy was Wilson Mitchell, a successful businessman from Chester, Pennsylvania. The guy was seeking the Republican nomination for the state's First District seat in Congress. It was his second run for public office, and Partridge's contact guy told him that Mitchell was spending unusually large amounts of his personal money on the campaign. Partridge felt nothing much stuck out about him but was excited about his second lead. The second lead concerned a guy who lived in Mississippi, and a conversation with the local newspaper editor, a Jerry Statford, proved to be very interesting.

"Lot of interest around this part of the country about

that race," said Statford. "In fact, there's some stuff happening as we speak. The local cable ran an ad that calls your guy Roger Mitchell unethical after pending federal racketeering charges levied against him were uncovered. Appears a former associate agreed to testify against him. Could get ugly in the next couple of months. Don't know if that's of any help, but feel free to call if you need more information. Assume you've visited his website for all his specifics—age, family, experience, that kind of stuff. Hey, how's it going up there on Cape Cod? Didn't I read that you guys had a hurricane?"

"We're fine here—just had some minor damage," said Partridge. "It was our neighbors to the south, New York and New Jersey, who got killed. Thanks for asking and thanks for the information. I'll be in touch if it pans out."

Cotter and Partridge compared notes. "Not a hell of a lot here," said Cotter. "Should we hold onto the list just in case?"

"It's probably a waste of time, but we've nothing to lose. I kind of like the sound of this Roger Mitchell—federal racketeering charges and some guy willing to testify against him. I say we bark up that tree first and find out anything that could link him to the Rafferty woman. You know, whether he ever lived or worked in any of the locations we're able to place her. We've got some pretty good information on her whereabouts through the years from her diaries. And, of course, we need to keep her age in mind as well as the age of this Mitchell guy."

"Thanks for the warning about their ages, Dick Tracy," said Cotter. "I'll keep that in mind. So what tree are you barking up?"

"Ah," laughed Partridge. "Afraid I won't be working as hard as you. Good to know you're keeping close tabs on me. Is that for your benefit or the chief's? Maybe you're even getting extra bucks for monitoring me. Never would have expected that from you."

They both laughed and got to work. Cotter worked on the Roger Mitchell angle. Partridge, working on a hunch, went back to take a second look at the rejected list of politicians with a first or last name of Mitchell.

CHAPTER 32

Judy waited until they were back in the car before grumbling to Phil. Dinner at Siena had been a mixed bag for her. "I know you probably won't agree with me, but it seems like the entire evening was about Mary and the murder. I think that was a little insensitive of everyone, don't you? They knew I wanted to relax and think about something else for a few hours."

"Is that a question?" said Phil. "If it is, then maybe the answer is you never stopped them. I never heard you tell them even once that tonight you'd rather not discuss the murder. I never heard you tell them it's still difficult to talk about the murder. In fact it seems to me that you were as involved in the conversation as everyone else. Really Judy, . . . think about it. A murder happened in our community, and the victim wasn't simply a neighbor. She was someone you had come to love who turned out to be your aunt. What do you expect of your friends? If the tables were turned, and one of your friends was involved, you'd be asking the same questions."

"I knew you wouldn't agree. And then to tell me that it was my fault—my God Phil, sometimes I wonder about you. You know it would be nice if you saw my point of view once in a while. Who am I supposed to talk to about my feelings if you end up taking the other side? When your mother was alive, and you and I discussed her feelings and her complaints, you always said we should just listen and not comment because we'd only aggravate her further if we tried to explain the other side of an issue."

"Oh now you're comparing yourself to my mother. She was ninety years old and living in a nursing home. She was miserable, and she was sick. It would have accomplished nothing to have tried to have a discussion with her. You aren't old, and you aren't sick. And, you aren't in a nursing home. So don't mix my mother into this conversation. Sometimes I get sick and tired of your criticism of other people. People are people. That's the way they are. Sometimes they think, and sometimes they don't. Most people can only see things from their perspective, so give your friends some slack. They're involved in what happened. Of course not as much as you, but the murder did take place in their community, too. Don't forget that, and he let out an audible sigh."

Judy didn't respond. Instead she turned away from Phil and stared out the car's side window and groaned just loud enough for him to hear. The ride home passed without another word spoken by either one of them. Judy went to her bedroom as soon as they got home. She was in a funk and wanted to be left alone. The phone rang as she was about to get comfortable and try to concentrate enough to read her new book. She answered out of habit and without looking at the caller's name. Shirley was on the other end.

"Judy, are you okay?" Shirley said. "I mean . . . you seemed a little quiet this evening, not that anyone else necessarily noticed, and I wanted to make sure you were okay. Tonight when everyone was talking all about Mary and why someone would want to kill her and about her astonishing life, I glanced over at you a few times, and you looked kind of weird. I mean not weird but maybe not totally focused on all of us and what we were talking about, so I wanted to check on you. I mentioned it to Chuck, and he said it was my imagination. If it was my imagination, ignore me and throw it up to my concern for a good friend."

Judy began to cry and told Shirley about her conversation with Phil.

"Don't you cry over what Phil said, honey. You know men. They don't have a sensitive bone in them most of the time, and they certainly aren't good at picking up subtleties. So put that conversation out of your head. It's not worth your tears."

"Thanks, Shirley. You're a good friend. I understand why everyone wants to talk about Mary, but sometimes I want to think about something else. It's like living the horror over and over again. I mean it's not just that Mary died, and I'm in mourning. It's so much worse than that. It's the sight of her bloodied body in the bathtub that I can't stop seeing. No matter what people are talking about, that's the vision in my head. I'm sure in time it will be easier, but right now it's too soon. I'm glad they found the guy who killed her, but I wish I knew why he did what he did. The whole thing doesn't make any sense."

"I'm glad I called you," said Shirley. "Just try and remember the book *Men Are from Mars, Women Are from Venus*—they'll never understand us, and we'll never understand them. Now try to relax, and I'll talk to you tomorrow."

Phil knocked on the bedroom door. "Are you off the phone? Can I come in?"

"Sure . . . I guess."

"Are you going to talk to me now, or are you still brooding?"

"I don't want to discuss tonight," she said. "I'm not brooding. I'm just tired. I thought it would help me to relax if I read before going to bed. And for your information—

that was Shirley on the phone, and she agreed with me. So I know I'm not crazy. Let's just say we agree to disagree and drop the whole thing. You understand tonight your way, and I understand it my way. Are you watching television or are you going to read in bed too?"

"Probably television. The recap of the football game is on, and you know I can never get enough. If you go to bed before me, set the alarm for seven. I'm supposed to meet Larry for breakfast over at Panera's." With that last comment he said, "Love you," and he shut the bedroom door.

CHAPTER 33

He was reading a news article on his computer when he saw a brief headline at the bottom of the screen. Something caused him to open the link, and he was stunned when he saw the woman's picture. Although she had a different name in the article, he was sure she was the same woman from his time in Vegas, the one he had searched for and even put a hit out on years earlier to no avail. He had not thought about her for years. His first thought was to call Nelson.

"Hey, Nelson, hope you're sitting down. Guess what I found today. Remember the crazy girl, Shirley Nichols, who was that guy Smitty's girlfriend? You know, the guy who was our bouncer a million years ago at the Pink Coin, and then the Sands, before we had him put away for squealing. Seems someone knocked her off somewhere in Massachusetts, of all places. And get this ... Santiago, that loser, supposedly did it."

"What! You've got to be shitting me," said Nelson.

"I'm not kidding. And the article said Santiago was shot during a stand-off based on some anonymous tip. Can you believe this? I wonder how the hell he found her after all these years, and why he killed her? What did he expect to gain? It's crazy. We tried to find her years ago, remember? We even put out a hit with a substantial reward.

Both of us always thought she learned about the casino heists and the prostitute deaths from her boyfriend Smitty, and that was why she ran. But now, now after all these years—my God, it must be thirty or more years ago—and now she turns up. This is insane, really insane. They're both dead, so I doubt anything will come our way from this, but I called to give you a heads up. Let me know if you hear anything, and I'll do the same. Hey, now that we're talking, how's it going in your world? We haven't seen one another for ages. No room in Vegas now for small potatoes like us. Not like the old days. Now it's the big guys and big corporations. Hell, I hate being old. You know, we should get together for lunch and reminisce. Call when you have some time; just wanted to say stay alert," and he hung up.

He read the article again, unable to understand the whole situation, but he didn't see anything he hadn't seen the first time. To play it safe, he put out a Google alert to notify him if anything else appeared in the news. "What the hell, probably nothing will come of this," he said to himself. But he now had that itchy feeling in the pit of his stomach he always got when he was nervous.

"You alright?" she asked him that night at dinner. "You've been jumpy all day like you just saw a ghost. You want to tell me what's yanking your chain, or do you want to just stew about it?"

He hated the way his wife always saw right through him. He could usually waltz around her accusations and tell her she was crazy, but this time he knew she had him. "God," he thought, "was it that obvious?" He knew he needed to calm down before she pushed him any further. If anything came of Sheila's murder, and they questioned him, he needed to have his act together. He made himself a drink, lit up a cigar, and thought about his options if he was ever confronted by the police.

CHAPTER 34

Cotter worked much of the early morning hours on the Roger Mitchell connection and Mitchell's pending federal racketeering charges. Mitchell even had his own website. Later in the morning Cotter reviewed his findings with Partridge.

"This one's quite a guy," said Cotter. "Don't know how they get away with running for office when they have shit like this in their background, but here's everything I found. Appears the guy held some low level positions in county government, ran a few times for some state positions, and is currently the local election commissioner."

"What the hell does a local election commissioner in Mississippi do?" laughed Partridge.

"Get this," said Cotter. "The guy's responsible for conducting non-partisan elections, certifying election results, and cleaning up voter lists."

"You've got to be joking," said Partridge. "They really have a guy charged with federal racketeering in a position to certify election results and decide if people have the right to vote? What's wrong with them down in good ole Miss? And wasn't there some controversy in Florida, another champion of voting rights, about voter lists?"

"Good memory," said Cotter. "Got a cousin down there who I talk to all the time about that kind of stuff.

Remember him telling me how they were hit with a slew of lawsuits after they lopped a couple hundred thousand names off their eligible voting lists."

"There's crazy stuff going on out there," said Partridge. "So what else did you find about our guy?"

"I traced everything I could—work experience, where he was raised, educational background, everything—and I checked out his website which, by the way, had this real slick link for donating money to his campaign."

"And . . . " said Partridge. "Jesus Christ, Cotter, why do I have to drag information out of you? Tell me about his work experience."

"I was about to, but you interrupted me," snapped Cotter.

"Sure, sure, so tell me."

"Well, seems he was a longshoreman down in the Port of Gulfport. So he's evidently in the union or he wouldn't have been allowed to do that sort of work."

"Sounds like our guy has quite the interesting background. What did you say the specifics were of his racketeering charges?" asked Partridge.

"The guy is accused of taking campaign contributions in exchange for political favors, which I guess isn't that unusual in today's world," said Cotter. "Seems making false statements is the only indictment against him that's holding, but his lawyer says the guy didn't fully understand the information he was being asked to provide. You know, the usual crap."

"I think it's time we contact the locals down there and maybe question this guy," said Partridge. "Let's talk to the chief and see if we can fly down. I'm still looking at the list of suspects we rejected, but I like this Roger Mitchell."

"You're shitting me, right?" yelled Yablonski. "My budget is being cut by the town manager all the time, and you want me to live with even less because you want to go to Mississippi on a hunch. Give me a break! Arrange a Skype interview or do Facetime, whatever. But the answer is no unless you want to pay for this yourself."

"A Skype interview—now that's interesting," smiled Partridge. "Is that something new the courts are allowing?"

"You know it's allowed," yelled Yablonski. "Now get the hell out of here and shut my door on your way out."

The interview was arranged for later that day after much haggling about the best time because Mitchell, according to his lawyer, was a very busy person. The guy claimed no knowledge of anyone by the name of Sheila Nichols, Mary Rafferty, or Jack Santiago. "Never worked in the Vegas area, never had dealings there, and not associated with anyone in the area," he told them. "Check my background, my records, my business dealings, anything you want . . . you won't find a damn thing. You've got the wrong guy. I'm clean, so go bother someone else. I have a campaign to run here."

With that, they were back to square one.

"Damn!" said Partridge. "Let's review what we know. The Francheska woman said Santiago was planning to blackmail a politician by the name of Mitchell, no first name and no location. If Santiago knew him from Vegas, I say we contact Vegas and see if their records go back far enough to come up with the name of a Mitchell in any connection. He might not have been a politician back then. It's a needle in a haystack, but right now I think it's our best bet unless you have a bright idea."

"I'm up against a wall just like you," said Cotter.

"Go see if you can hit the end of your daughter's soccer game," said Partridge. "Me, I need a drink and some thinking time. See you tomorrow, and hopefully one of us will come up with something by then."

CHAPTER 35

He was still involved in illegal dealings, but he was smarter these days and very rarely had any trouble with the cops. He no longer ran with his old friends, his brother had stopped talking to him years ago, and his parents were long dead. He was quite respectable now. He had a home, a wife, three kids, four grandchildren, and a successful limo business. He had run back then with Sarno, the mastermind behind Vegas. Sarno had used his friendship with teamster boss Jimmy Hoffa and teamster backing to build Caesar's Palace and Circus Circus. Sarno and Hoffa were both dead, but he was still around. He rarely spoke to the old guys. Some were in the slammer, some had retired to the good life, and some were dead. But this blast from the past was troubling him. He poured himself a scotch and puffed on his cigar, but it was not relaxing him. Nelson hadn't sounded worried when they spoke, but Nelson had always been a laid-back guy.

Life back then had been so different. The money had been rolling, and he had had his choice of women, cars and vacations. He had had it all. But that life was over. Now he didn't have to worry about a knock on the door or continually look out his rear view mirror to see if the cops were following him. Anne Marie took him in when he got out of prison. She met him at the super market where she worked as a cashier, and they began to date on a very casual basis—just coffee or a quick sandwich during her lunch hour. When they began to spend more time together, he told her about himself and his prison record. She seemed to take it in stride. Now all that was history. Of course the three kids and the four grandchildren were from her first marriage, but they treated him as if he had always been part of the family. The limo business gave them money beyond her small salary, and life was good. He began to sweat as he thought about what could happen if Santiago's stupidity brought all of this to a crashing halt. He took a swig of his drink, tried to calm down, and turned on the football game. He had bet a few bucks on the Jets and was hoping for a big win.

CHAPTER 36

Partridge called Cynthia and hoped that she did not have plans for the evening; he missed her when they were not together. He tried to keep a respectful distance in deference to her kids, and so her brother, Chief Yablonski, would not lecture him about their relationship. So far it had been great. There were dinners together while a babysitter watched the kids, and even long drives around the Cape with all of them. Sometimes he would even go to the kids' games and do a bit of coaching.

Cynthia answered the phone and sounded excited to hear his voice. "Hey you, I didn't think you'd call until later tonight. I thought you said you'd be working long hours trying to solve the murder case over at Northridge. Does this call mean you solved it?"

"Wish it meant that," and he laughed. "No, still working and still thinking, but I told Cotter I needed a chance to get away from the case for a bit. You know— maybe if I get away for a while the change might spark a few neurons and result in one of my brilliant hunches. Need one of those real bad right now cause I've been coming up real empty," and he laughed again.

"Do you want to come over later or maybe out for a drink and a bite?" she said. "I'm open to either or even just a long talk on the phone. Whatever works for you. I just need to first feed the kids, help with homework, and then put them to bed."

"How about out for a drink and a bite?" he said. "I'd really like that. Can you get someone last minute to watch the kids?"

"Sure, probably the girl across the street. She can always use the money, and she told me she's usually available during the week."

"Name a time, and I'll be there," he said. "Where do you want to go or should I pick?"

"Why don't you pick. I think it's your turn anyway," and she laughed.

"Are you keeping track of this? You're keeping track aren't you? That's so funny. I won't tell anyone. It'll be our secret."

"Now who's being funny?" and she thought she could see a smile spread across his face. "How about Trevi? I love that place, and they have small plates which work for me late at night."

"Great, how does 8:30 sound?"

They sat at a high top on the bar side of the restaurant. It was a quiet night, and no one bothered them as they continued to relax with a glass of wine long after they had finished with their food.

"Cynth, I can't tell you how awesome this is to relax with someone special after a hard day at the station. I'm trying to get a handle on this case, but it's not coming together for me. I've no good leads and no real hunches. I know I'm looking straight at something, but I don't know what it is. I keep going over and over the facts. I'm hoping that I'll dream about something tonight to set me on the right course," and he laughed.

She was good for him. He could feel it in every part of his existence, and could not believe how relaxed he felt and how strong his feelings for her were right at that moment.

He had been thinking about her day and night for months, and somehow today, tonight, right this very moment felt like the right time to get serious. Just thinking about what he was about to say made him smile.

"Why are you smiling?" she said. "Do you want to let me in on why you're smiling?"

"Yup," and then he grinned from ear to ear like a silly kid. He reached for her hand and said, "The more time we spend together, the more I miss you when you're away from me. I can't expect you to stay in a relationship that isn't going anywhere. You deserve a husband and a father for your children. I think I can provide that for you, but I want you to know sometimes I get scared. My one experience as a cop and husband was pretty disastrous. I don't want a repeat of my last marriage. If you'll gamble on me, and if you feel about me the way I feel about you, I'd like to ask you to marry me. That's if you'll have me?"

She began to cry. "Of course I'll have you, and of course I feel the same way about you. I've always dreamt of meeting someone for me and for the kids, but I never thought I'd ever find anyone as awesome and wonderful as you," and she began to cry again. "I love you so much. You're so thoughtful. The kids love you, and you're so good with them. Oh my God, wait until my brother hears. He'll go crazy you know. At first he'll be happy for me, and then he'll realize that he'll no longer be just Chief Yablonski to you. Now he'll also be your grouchy brother-in-law. We have to tell him together so we can both see his expression. It'll be a riot," and she giggled.

"One other thing," he said. "I want you to have this ring. It's not the actual engagement ring . . . I want you to pick that one out because I know ring tastes are a personal thing. This ring belonged to my grandmother, and I want you to have it. It'll probably fit on your little finger. I know you well enough to know that this ring will mean as much to you as it does for me to give it to you. So, if we're both finished crying, I say we get out of here."

As they left the restaurant, he spotted a discarded copy of the day's newspaper. He picked it up, quite unaware of its significance, and threw it in his car.

CHAPTER 37

"Is Cotter in yet?" Partridge said to the dispatcher.

"Yup, got in a few minutes ago."

Partridge made his way down the corridor to their small office. He had been promised a better office when he first joined the Marshland Police Department, but nothing had ever come of the promise. "There you are," he said with a lilt in his voice.

"Boy you sound chipper this morning," said Cotter. "You get laid or something?"

"Cut the wise cracks and listen. I've got a hunch. I read this in yesterday's Reporter," and he showed Cotter a newspaper article from the paper he picked up the night before.

"So what does this have to do with us and our case? I don't get it."

"Cotter, you have no insights, no imagination, and no ability to be open to a hunch. This, my friend, is a possible new direction for our investigation. Maybe we're looking for the wrong guy. Maybe we need to find a guy like the one in this article."

"You think?" said Cotter.

"Yah, I think. Let's go back and seriously look at that list of politicians named Mitchell that we rejected as not pertinent. I say we contact them and ask questions about their background. If we come up with anything, then we can go back and ask more specific questions."

After a couple of hours of trying to get the right people on the phone or get the right people to call them back, Cotter found a guy he thought might fit Partridge's hunch.

"Hey Partridge," he said, "maybe this is the guy. I couldn't talk to him, but someone in his campaign said there have always been rumors about just such a thing. Wouldn't give me his name. Said he didn't want to get into trouble with the candidate for spreading gossip. I did get him to tell me, however, the name of the person to speak with if we wanted to follow up on this line of questioning. What do you think?"

"I don't think. Dammit, I know. I can feel it. This is the guy who's going to help us tie up the case. Yup, this is the guy."

"Hold on cowboy. Slow down," said Cotter. "You may be right, but aren't you a little over the top this morning? Are you sure you didn't get laid last night?"

"Shut up and give me the number and the guy's name. And for your information, last night is none of your business."

The guy they wanted to speak with was a Jason Mitchell running for the State Senate in Vermont. Partridge was thrilled that the guy was local. He hoped they would be able to drive up to Vermont, rather than question the guy over the phone. He liked to look a guy straight in the eye when questioning him.

They found the chief in his office and explained their request. The chief liked the sound of what they were after and granted them the time to drive to Montpelier, Vermont. Partridge spoke with Mitchell's administrative assistant, explained who he was, and made arrangements to speak with the candidate Jay Mitchell later that day.

"So detectives, I understand you're interested in some

information about my brother Jerome. I'm surprised you discovered that I have a brother. Haven't seen or heard anything about him since we were kids. He always ran with a tough crowd in high school, and I was always the student. We hated each other. My folks used to plead with us to be civil, but we never listened. We went our separate ways right after graduation; actually, he didn't graduate. My folks died in a traffic accident during my junior year of college. I didn't know how to contact my brother, and there was nothing in my folk's papers that gave me a clue about where to find him. He had basically rejected the entire family and vanished. I've been a corporate lawyer for most of my life, and this is my first run for office. I guess I could have tried to find him, but to tell you the truth, I didn't care. We had a very small family. My father was an only child, and my mother's sister never married. So no cousins and no one to wonder about my long lost brother until today. Why are you looking for him? Did he commit a crime or something?"

They got the information they needed and thanked Jay Mitchell for his time and his forthrightness in helping them. Their next task was to search the country for someone by the name of Jerome Mitchell who had a brother named Jay Mitchell. They began a laptop search as they made their way home from Montpelier.

There were a lot of Jerome Mitchells out there, and Partridge didn't want to spook the guy by confronting him on the phone. "This is my plan," he told Cotter. "See what you think. We each make calls saying we are the lawyer for the estate of Mildred and Frank Mitchell. We say that there is an inheritance to be split between living members of the family. We then try to ascertain if we have the right guy. Hopefully our guy will acknowledge a brother, and then bingo we'll have him. So, is it a plan?"

"Sounds like one to me boss," and Cotter laughed.

They began their search the next day, and it was Partridge who found the correct Jerome Mitchell. He was living in a small town in Idaho. He was married and the owner of a one man limo service. Partridge assured him that he would be mailing out the necessary paper work to begin the inheritance process.

"Chief, we've got the right guy," said Partridge with a sense of satisfaction. "The guy clarified his relationship to our politician when we told him an inheritance was due him if he was the correct Jerome Mitchell. Didn't hesitate. Told us everything we needed. We're asking to go up to his place in Idaho, confront him, question him, and if necessary bring him back here. Do we have your go ahead?"

They were on their way to Idaho the next day.

"I've never been to Idaho, have you? I mean who goes to Idaho?" said Cotter while munching on the peanuts and chips handed out by the stewardess.

"I can't believe you like this junk," said Partridge while looking aghast at Cotter. "You can have mine too if you want. Me, I'm watching the waist. Wouldn't be a bad idea if you did the same cause I'm noticing something there under your shirt. Do you want to tell me about that baby bump?" and he laughed.

"Cut the crap. A little run and a few pushups, and it'll be gone. I'm not a great flyer, and eating calms me down. I start to think about lost flights and someone taking over the plane, and I get the heebie jeebies. And with this turbulence, well yup I'll take those extra chips and nuts, and no I'm not one of those pregnant guys. Hey, did you see the story about a guy who was in the process of switching to a male body from a female one? His operations or hormones or whatever weren't finished, his wife couldn't carry a baby, and so he carried the baby. Strangest thing I ever saw. He was a male in every way from his outward appearance. Made the round of talk shows and all. Crazy world."

"Nope, didn't see it," said Partridge. "And yes, I've been to Idaho. Did a cross country trip with a bunch of kids when I was straight out of college. We were in Montana and Wyoming and then we cut over to Idaho. One of the guys had an aunt there, and we did some hiking. Went to Bruneau Dunes State Park to a place called Perrine Bridge, or something like that. It was near the Snake River. I remember we drove across a bridge into Twin Falls, but it was October and there wasn't much to see because the falls in the area were dry. You know, not much water flow. My friend was happy, though, because he got to spend a couple of days with this aunt, but I wasn't impressed after everything else we had seen. And now here I am in Idaho again."

They were met at the airport by a Detective Albert from Emmett. He had agreed to accompany them to question Jerome Mitchell. The detective said he knew Mitchell, whom he called Jay. "Everyone knows Jay," he said. "We're a small town, so everyone knows everyone. I'd be surprised if he's the guy you're looking for, but maybe. People move into town, we don't do a computer search to find out about them. They are who they want to be, but Jay sure does match your guy. Hope not; he's a great guy. Played softball with him back a few years. Well, let's find out."

It was a short ride from the airport to the guy's home. The detective knocked on the door and explained their visit. Partridge and Cotter gasped when they saw him. He was the spitting image of his brother. They were identical twins. The politician hadn't said his brother was a twin. The pieces were beginning to fall into place.

"Jay," Detective Albert said, "these detectives are here from Massachusetts about the murder of a Mary Rafferty formerly known as Sheila Nichols. They say a guy called

Santiago was responsible and that he had bragged he was going to blackmail a politician by the name of Mitchell, who had once offered a reward to anyone who found this Sheila Nichols and her diaries. So they'd like to talk to you about it. May we come in?"

Mitchell never denied knowing Sheila Nichols. "Yah, I knew Sheila. What does this have to do with me? I'm not a politican."

Cotter told Mitchell about notes they found in Mary Rafferty's diary describing her friend Smitty and his death. Then Partridge explained his theory.

"I think that Santiago was probably involved in this Smitty's death along with you," said Partridge. "I think that a short time ago Santiago saw a picture of your brother and learned he was running for office in Vermont. He thought it was you, and he planned to get rich blackmailing you. That's what this has to do with you."

"I'm not responsible for what that idiot Santiago thought. I didn't kill that woman, and I don't know anything about someone called Smitty. So my brother is running for office in Vermont. I'll be damned. Haven't thought about him since we were kids. Parents named me Jerome. Always hated the name. When I left home, I told everyone my name was Jay. The kid got the school brains and the better name of Jay. I got screwed. You've got nothing on me."

"Sorry, Jay," said Detective Albert. "Got to ask you to come down to the station for questioning. Too many pieces pointing your way. Sorry. I suggest you make it easy on yourself and come with me. Don't want to put on a show for the neighbors or your family if they happen to walk in on us."

Mitchell agreed to accompany Detective Albert to the station, where he was questioned and then booked on suspicion of involvement in the murder of Peter Smith, known as Smitty. He crumbled and implicated his friend Nelson whom he claimed was the actual hit man.

Cotter and Partridge discussed the case on their way back to Marshland. "Funny how a piece of mistaken information on the part of our guy Santiago led to the Rafferty woman's death and the solution to a long inactive case regarding this guy Smitty. Imagine, identical twins. Boy that sure was a shocker when the guy answered the door," laughed Cotter.

"Guess our gal Elsie might qualify for a reduced sentence based on the information she provided," said Partridge. "Doubt if she knew what she knew, but the result is still the same. Well, we pretty much cleared up that case and even got a trip to boot. So sit back, relax and enjoy your junk food and mine on the flight home."

"Hey," said Cotter, "don't forget that you promised to treat me to breakfast at Moonakis when this case was solved. So while I'm eating all this junk, I'm going to think about their delicious Swedish pancakes."

CHAPTER 38

"Get the phone," yelled Judy. "I'm in the middle of getting dressed. Tell whoever it is that I'll call them back later."

After a brief conversation, Phil went into their bedroom and told Judy about the phone call. "The guy on the phone wanted to interview you. Said he was a reporter for the *Cape Cod Times*. I said I was your husband and asked if I could help. He explained that the paper wanted to do a feature article about Mary Rafferty—her early life, her relation to you, and her diaries and how they led to her murder and the solution of an old unsolved murder in Vegas. They thought it would be a great human interest story. You know—how Mary, after all those years, helped to solve the murder of her friend Smitty and get those responsible put away for probably the rest of their lives."

"Too bad she had to give up her life in the process," said Judy. "A lot of information they probably want is personal. I don't know if I want it dragged through the paper with everyone talking about me."

"It's not about you," said Phil. "It's about Mary. If you don't give them the correct information, they might come up with material you don't want printed. Why don't you speak to the reporter and see if you can have final approval. That way you'll know that what they're printing is accurate."

"Now that it's over, I really don't want to talk about it anymore. It doesn't seem fair. This article will bring it all up again. I don't know if I want to go through all that."

"You can't stop the article. It's probably going to be written whether you agree to be interviewed or not, so you might as well get your two cents in," said Phil.

"You think?"

"Yes, I think. So finish getting dressed and call the guy back."

"You're probably right," she said. "When you're right you're right, but don't let my compliment go to your head. You're still wrong loads of times," and she laughed. "By the way, did I tell you that I love you?"

"Don't think you told me those exact words today," he said, "but I wouldn't mind hearing them."

She laughed and said, "You know, it's good to laugh once in a while. We should both try it more often!"

THE AUTHOR

Roberta Schneiderman grew up in Massachusetts and earned a graduate degree in special education. She taught for over twenty years at the high school level working with a learning disabled population. She is retired from teaching and currently spends her time between Cape Cod and Florida.

Ms. Schneiderman may be contacted through her publisher at **saltypilgrim.com**

Made in the USA
Columbia, SC
15 November 2017